HARLEM HUSTLE

HARLEM
HUSTLE

JANET McDONALD

FRANCES FOSTER BOOKS
FARRAR, STRAUS AND GIROUX
NEW YORK

YA
(1)

Library of Congress Cataloging-in-Publication Data
McDonald, Janet.
    Harlem Hustle / Janet McDonald.— 1st ed.
        p.   cm.
    Summary: Eric "Hustle" Samson, a smart and street-wise seventeen-year-old Harlem-born dropout, aspires to rap stardom, a dream he naively believes is about to come true.
    ISBN-13: 978-0-374-37184-5
    ISBN-10: 0-374-37184-9
    [1. Rap (Music)—Fiction.   2. African Americans—Fiction.   3. Harlem (New York, N.Y.)—Fiction.]   I. Title.

PZ7.M4784178 Har 2006
[Fic]—dc22

                                                    2005052108

"We Real Cool" by Gwendolyn Brooks reprinted by consent of Brooks Permissions. "Kissie Lee" from *This Is My Century: New and Collected Poems* by Margaret Walker reprinted by consent of The University of Georgia Press.

To those pen pals who find the words
to ask of me in so many words
to continue to put in these, my words,
their stories as lived in their own words.

ACKNOWLEDGMENTS

To my editor, Frances Foster, and my agent, Charlotte Sheedy, *un grand merci*. Much appreciation to Jeanne McDermott, Director of Marketing, for the laugh that shores my spirit and the props that revived this work; and to Sabeth Albert, Publicity Manager, for her dogged dedication to blowing me up, Boom!

Shouts go out to Paulie Jane, Annie Cat, Françoise, Honkea, adviser-at-large Colette Modiano, Passy homegirl Olivia, Salem's Special Karyn, Suzanne B., and Ginny from the Block.

And as always, greatest gratitude to my brother and fellow author, Kevin "Projectboy" McDonald, whose living inspires mine.

HARLEM HUSTLE

1

IN A BUSTLING MANHATTAN BOUTIQUE, THE GAME OF COPS and robbers was playing itself out with the heart-pounding tension of a bungee jump. Hustle glanced over his shoulder as he walked between racks of warm-up suits. He felt *off* somehow, unable to tell customers from cops. *Everybody* seemed to have that Five-O look, the darting eyes, the police academy swagger, the bad vibe.

For both the bungee jumper and the shoplifter, once the leap is taken, there's no turning back. The jumper can't defy gravity, and the thief, once spotted, can't elude security. But Hustle was determined to try. He slipped on a black velour sweat suit top, the price tag sticking out at his wrist, and ran his hands over the fabric. If there were any electronic tags hidden in the cloth, he was going to find and remove them. His theft-trained fingers felt something hard in the seam of the collar.

"Hey!"

Hustle spun around. A young guy in a dark blazer was watching, on his lapel the letters TSU for Times Square Urbanwear, a boutique that not only clothed hip-hop stars but carried their personal brands of overpriced gear and accessories. The store also sold its own fashions under the label GangstaThreads.

"Hey *what*?" Hustle's body tensed as he spoke the words. This wouldn't be the first time he'd fought off store security. And this skinny dude, he was sure he could handle.

"All those sweats are on sale, but some of the tags still show the old prices. Just so you know."

The sales assistant moved on. Hustle wiped sweat from his eyebrows and hung up the outfit. He thought he saw another guy, tall and bald, scoping him but decided it was just paranoia.

Hustle wandered from one aisle to another, squeezing past shoppers. He circled tables piled high with designer underwear. The store resounded with rap music and cell phone conversations. Like a foul-line shooter tuning out the opposing team's noisy supporters, Hustle heard nothing when he was working. Almost nothing could shake his concentration. Except girls.

Three caught his eye. They seemed to be doing more

loitering than shopping. TSU had become a hangout for penniless project girls hoping to meet stars. And this unholy trinity was undoubtedly straight outta the hood, with their pink and black braided extensions and provocative attitude. Dishin' and dissin', they shouted over the pulsing beats of Ciara's latest hit.

"Oh, check *this* one out. And that *hair*, it's irkin' my nerves! How somebody that dark gon' be a blonde? She ain't even *trynna* make it look real."

"Truuue! She *need* to be buying husself some new clothes 'cause no she *di'ent* come out the house wearing them more-Parks-Sausages pants." It was interesting that the girl speaking was quite a bit chunkier than the blonde.

"Oh yes she *did*, guuurl, and that panty line . . . it's cuttin' *deep* in that butt! What's all that she heistin' anyway? TSU do *not* take food stamps."

The girls laughed rowdily, giving high fives all around. Hustle had just picked up a white suede hoodie when the blonde in question bumped into him. In her arms she carried a mound of clothes.

"Oops, 'scuse me!" She giggled in a way that made Hustle wonder if the collision was really an accident.

"No problem, shorty." Her eyes held his for a brief moment. The reaction a few feet away was less charitable.

"Oh no she *di'ent* walk dead into him on purpose with that doll hair weave!"

"Guuurl, no you *di'ent* say 'doll hair weave'! You need to stop before you make me fall out on the flo' laughin'!"

"Yes, I most definitely *did*, and if she don't peel them beady eyeballs off me, I'ma go from sayin' to doin'!"

The girls were *rolling*, tears in their eyes. The blonde glared at her insulters. Then she rolled her eyes as slow and hard as she could and walked away.

Hustle laughed. Girls could be *crazy* nasty, hatin' on each other at first sight. For no reason. At least a dude always had a reason. Of course, if they had been dudes, somebody would've already been bleeding. Still, he'd rather be beat down with a fist than tore down with a dis. Toe-to-toe, he could hold his own in a brawl with anybody, but words could put more of a hurtin' on a dude than anything.

Hustle had long ago recognized the power of words. They had drawn him as a boy to rap music. When he was in the fourth grade, he found a rhyming dictionary in the school library and wrote his first rap. The kid fantasy later blossomed into a young man's dream. Whether he would stay on the path to make that dream a reality was uncertain. An early detour had already taken a nightmarish turn.

Boosting was all he knew, and he'd been one of the best because he loved it so—the challenge, the adrenaline, and, of course, the money.

He'd started young, after quitting junior high, and had the gift of invisibility. Uniformed guards, plainclothes agents, store personnel, no one ever seemed to see the oddly bulky little boy. As his skills developed, he could leave a store wearing three shirts and a pair of pants under his own clothes without a bulge in sight. His specialization was S & S, a technique of switching and substituting old clothes for new ones. He took orders uptown and filled them downtown. Neighbors called him "Harlem's professional shopper." His famous boast was that he could move merchandise with one eye open. But be they celebrities seeking thrills or hustlers making a living, shoplifters eventually are caught, and the day came when Hustle wished he'd kept *both* eyes open.

Maybe if he hadn't played hooky the day NYPD guest speakers visited his school he would've learned about advances in store security. And maybe he wouldn't have walked past the sensors of the Leather Outfitter wearing a beautiful royal blue leather bomber he hadn't paid for. And maybe he wouldn't have been exposed by that soft sensor tag embedded in the jacket's lining. But none of these *maybes* happened, and Hustle was busted, booked, and jailed.

He'd been arrested before and always let go with a warning, thanks to fake names and a baby face. This time he slipped and gave the same false name he'd given once before. That matchup led to a second match, which led to the truth, and soon Eric Samson and all his aliases were known to the police. Arguing with great skill and truthlessness, his lawyer, Olivia Sigal, negotiated a sentence of probation for misdemeanor larceny. Not, however, before Hustle had spent his seventeenth birthday behind bars, awaiting trial. Shaken by what he'd seen angry men on lockdown do to one another, he made one of those never-again promises people make to themselves in the dark moments of their lives only to blithely abandon with the first rays of sunlight.

Within months of his release he'd followed his desire for easy money back to the doorstep of that same darkness, and entered Times Square Urbanwear, where shoppers zipped up zippers, unbuttoned buttons, and fingered fabric. They bounced and bobbed to the music, some singing along. Hustle held a burgundy fleece jogging suit against his body, running his hands over it for cut and quality. A girl had her eyes on him. He felt them but pretended not to. She looked too young to be undercover, he thought, but you never know. Suddenly she was right there.

"I like how you feeling on that top," she said in a flirty voice.

"Oh yeah?" he answered. Rubbing his chin, he looked her up and down. "When you in the, um, clothing business like me, you gotta be able to *feeel.* Everything." He was close enough to smell her perfume.

"*Ooooo,*" she breathed.

"Like this," he said, touching her hair, "nice . . ." Her giggles spurred him on. "You know that Mario song about love?"

"Sheree!" A bull of a woman stomped towards them. "If you don't get your fresh tail"—she gave her daughter's arm a ferocious yank—"away from that—" Hustle stepped back from the woman's blazing glare. "Cain't you see she ain't nuthin' but a chile of thirteen? Ain't got a *drop* of decency, not a *one* of y'all!" She whacked the girl's head and dragged her away. "Just you wait till I get you home!"

2

HUSTLE JOSTLED HIS WAY THROUGH THE CLUSTERS OF shoppers gathered at the sales tables. He roamed upstairs to the sneakers department, then back down. He studied an oversized black T-shirt with BIG UP BIGGIE, R.I.P. scrawled graffiti-style under the jowly face of the dead rapper. He wanted it and tried to convince himself he could do a swift roll and stick without anyone noticing. But unwelcome memories floated into his head. The judge's warning that there'd be no probation next time. Some people, no matter how tough, just can't endure the crowded solitude of jail. Thick steel doors pin them tight against their limits. Small barred windows box off the once-open sky. Narrow bunks hold them aloft in unbreathable air. During those few months inside, Hustle was snatched awake each night by his own fear. He couldn't return to jail.

He folded the T-shirt, placed it back on the table. Touching his eyebrow, he stole a look between his fingers. Sure enough, the same tall guy he'd noticed before just happened to be a table away. What was his *deal*? Usually, Hustle could *feel* a cop, but this NBA reject was so obvious he wasn't sure *what* he was about.

The detective shadowing Hustle towered over the rows of metal racks hung with leather coats, bomber jackets, and oversized T-shirts. Low tables that barely reached the man's knees were piled high with baggy jeans, basketball jerseys, and midriff tank tops. From his perch atop legs so endless they belonged on a basketball court, he surveyed the store like a bird of prey keeping watch over its nest, ready to swoop and clutch any violator.

Hustle checked the price of a pair of baggies he liked. Two hundred fifty dollars for a pair of jeans? These people must be stone out they minds. He draped the pants over his arm and made his move towards the dressing rooms. As if a movie director had yelled, "Action!" the detective strolled over to the collection of sunglasses and baseball caps next to those same rooms and busied himself at the mirror trying different caps. Hustle smirked. The guy *had* to be Five-O, tailing him the way he was. It was as though he could actually *feel* the man's eyes on his back, *pushing* him, *daring* him. Cool, he thought, and for the first time looked straight at the man, who did not avert his eyes. The sucka dared test him? Cool.

"How many?" asked the attendant.

"Just one, my man. How you doin'?"

"Um, it be all good . . . my man." For reasons known only to himself, the boy blushed the same rich color as the lettering on his EMCEE DREW—TRAINEE badge. Perhaps he was embarrassed by his awkward use of Ebonics, a verbal style management encouraged as a way for employees to connect with their hip-hop clientele. Or he might have been affected by the emotion of dealing directly with his first shoplifting suspect, which he knew from the detective's secret signal. A larger than normal amount of blood passed through Drew's skin, coloring his neck, ears, and face rosy red. The detective looked at Drew in the mirror and mouthed angrily, "Act natural, goddammit!"

The trainee simply couldn't control his eyes, which shifted back and forth between Hustle and the detective. He did manage to verify that there was only a single pair of jeans, and not one tucked inside another. He handed Hustle a large red plastic pistol marked "1."

"Give . . . uh . . . a holler out if you need help. I'll be chilly right out here."

"No problem," said Hustle. "You da man."

Drew was red as a sunset.

• • •

Hustle stepped into what looked and smelled like a boys' locker room. Boys clad only in underwear posed and gawked at themselves in front of smudged mirrors, their flat chests hairless and sunburned. A kid wearing a white do-rag that was slightly too large for his smallish head stared at Hustle. The only clothing he had on was a pair of red boxer shorts patterned with little blue and white sailboats so wrinkled they resembled shipwrecks.

"Holy sh— You're . . . ! This is so feverish! Are you . . . ?"

"Yeah, homey, he be me and I be he. Wassup?"

He slapped hands with the boy, having no idea who he was being mistaken for but enjoying his fake fame.

The fan grabbed at his chest as though to slow down his heart. "Whoa, this is like *too* sick. I *love* your raps, dude, I *live* by them. Word is *bond*, Money!" Then he did something that he probably wouldn't have had he been able to see himself in the mirror. He closed his eyes and began bobbing up and down like a pale and sickly creature lost at sea. Other boys gathered around in Gangsta-Thread jeans and listened.

All the kids in my school, treat me like I'm a fool
'Cause my idols all rap, and the rest is all crap
Hip-hop is the sole tool, turn your life into a jewel
Like my boy Furius, who first wrecked then he ruled.

He opened his eyes slowly. "I wrote that for you last spring break."

So *that* was who this kid thought he was, Hustle realized, that chump Furius, who was about as fresh as stale hero bread in a bodega. The only thing that phony ever wrecked was his makeup when he fell in the pool at a BET video shoot.

The kid's performance was about as strange a thing as Hustle had ever seen. To say something, he asked the boy's name.

"Elias Watts Cromwell! But my rap name's Pimp-squeak."

Hustle laughed his rapper laugh. "*Heh heh*, that's *kickin'*, dawg. You keep keepin' it real, G-style."

The fan was elated. "Straight up ghetto fo' shizzle," he said. "So like what's the bizzle on your next album?"

"*What?* Where you get *them* vowels?"

"From Snoop," he answered as if talking about a personal friend. "MTV Cribizzle."

Hustle wasn't even about no Dogg-talk. They could keep that ghetto pig Latin on the West Coast.

"You know what, man, my time is *real* tight right now, so I'ma duck in here and check out these jeans. Later, Pimp."

Hustle found a booth, pulled shut the curtain, and sat down heavily on the wooden seat. In the back of his mind he knew it was crazy to try to lift *anything* with that detective stalking him. Even the greenest booster knew better than to tempt fate. Still, he felt like he had something to prove to himself—that he hadn't lost his touch. But his anxiety wasn't about lost touch, it was about losing his nerve.

A hand pulled open the curtain.

"Sorry, dude! Thought it was free!"

The same hand quickly closed it. The panic he felt in that instant shut down his brain, and pure instinct took over. The best boosters all had one thing in common— they knew when to give it up. Hustle left the booth, holding the jeans in his hand.

3

WORD HAD SPREAD THAT A FAMOUS RAPPER WAS SOME- where in the store. Kids eyed one another. Maybe it was him. Or *him*. A few had a general description. The detective was also on the lookout for Hustle, but for other reasons. He waited with Drew outside the dressing rooms. In a low voice, he explained to the trainee that with these guys, money had nothing to do with stealing. Rappers often deliberately get arrested—for the free publicity. They know their record company lawyers will get them off, and in the meantime they've reminded the whole country who they are. He'd seen it a million and one times, even right there at TSU.

Hustle appeared. Drew blushed. The detective watched.

"You taking them? Not *taking*, I mean, um, did they fit?" blurted the trainee, forgetting his diversity language instruction.

Hustle smiled directly at the detective. "They fit fine, but I ain't takin' 'em . . . this time."

Hustle wandered around the busy main section of the store as the trainee hastily examined the jeans to make sure everything was as it should be. It was the same pair, and the antitheft tags were still in place. He sighed with relief and nodded at the detective, who gave him a job-well-done wink.

Robert Burns wrote that the best laid plans of mice and men oft go astray, which today would roughly translate to, shit happens. As Hustle passed the jewelry counter, an unexpected moment of chaos allowed a crime to occur that Drew and the detective were certain they had prevented.

Some of the boys who'd been in the dressing room at the same time as Hustle now fluttered around him like excited doves. He gave high fives and scribbled illegible autographs. Pimpsqueak, who looked even skinnier with clothes *on*, had written his rap on a page from his spiral notebook, its edge shredded like the hem of an old slip.

"For you, Furius."

Lashondé, Kwalanna, and Tyreesha, the three project girls who'd also been eagerly waiting, could barely believe their eyes. The dude people were flocking around was so *not* Furius. Their wrath fell upon the person they held responsible for the disappointment—Elias Watts Cromwell.

"Boy, you need to take your bony butt back to Scarsdale or Riverdale or wherever the hell *dale* it come from," sneered one. "I know we all look alike to y'all, but that ain't Furius!"

"Heh heh," laughed Hustle.

Her friends were just as indignant but chose Hustle to vent on.

"Ain't *nuthin'* funny 'bout it. You got us waitin' up in here like a damn fool for your *frontin'* ass when we got *much* better things we could be doin'!"

"Truuue! And how you gon' play us like that *anyway,* when you don't look *nuthin'* like him? Furius got good hair, and he light-skinned!"

Like flies to a Kool-Aid spill, people from all over the store were drawn to the commotion near the front door. Then Pimpsqueak made two very wrong moves. First, he raised his hand the way he saw Justin Timberlake do to Ashton Kutcher when he got punked on *MTV Punk'd.* As if that gesture weren't bad enough, he then said something that would have been much better left unsaid.

"Yo, girl, talk to the hand! He *is* Furius, and it's like, if you don't know that, you have to be living in the dark ages or be on crack or something."

"Don't be puttin' your hand in my face!"

"Who you callin' *dark*?"

"Ya *mama* a crackhead!"

If they'd been dressed in silk loincloths with their hair in topknot buns, the trio could have passed for a women's sumo wrestling team. Circling Pimpsqueak, they were something even more intimidating—three very large, very tough, and very angry girls from Brooklyn's notorious Marcy Projects.

Now, it's well known that some people love to get a fight started, especially when it's not *their* faces, chests, and shins that are going to be scratched, punched, and kicked. For them it's just fun, like watching an action movie. One such person achieved exactly that when he, or she—no witness could or would identify the culprit— snatched off Pimpsqueak's do-rag and pushed him into Lashondé, who instinctively shoved him backward into the cheering spectators. Mayhem broke out. Kids were knocking over displays, crashing into mannequins, and running wild. A half dozen undercover cops instantly de- scended on them, including Alexa Norman, the blonde who'd "accidentally" bumped into Hustle, and the detec- tive, a former European league basketball player.

"Come on, break it up," they ordered. "Break it up, guys!"

Always alert for an opportunity and still smarting from his failure to lift the Biggie T-shirt or the jeans, Hus- tle pocketed a gold chain at the same moment Officer Norman was slapping cuffs on the flailing project girls.

4

HUSTLE WAITED A COUPLE OF DAYS BEFORE RETURNING TO Times Square. If once again his boosting nerve failed him, he could at least sell the chain he'd grabbed. Sidewalks swarmed with theatergoers, movie buffs, shoppers, and tourists. A handful of pickpockets and dealers loitered purposefully, survivors of the city's zero-tolerance anticrime program. Up and down the streets cars sped, buses maneuvered, taxis darted, and bike messengers dodged and swerved. In tunnels under the ground converged thirteen subway trains, and in the sky high above loomed giant billboards of steamy noodles, bubbly soft drinks, and wavy American flags.

Hustle slid through the crush of people with the ease

of a fish in familiar waters. He felt the weight of the chain in his pocket. The thought of that small victory made him smile. The memory of the havoc caused by his Furius impersonation made him laugh.

Chockablock with easily targeted shops, Times Square was a neighborhood Hustle knew as well as his own. He called it his "hood away from the hood." He moved through its streets with the blasé, unseeing eye of a New York native. But there was no way even *he* could overlook the latest addition to the visual circus—an eight-foot-tall, lace-clad beige colossus gracing the side of a building that stopped him in his tracks. He was making a detailed study of her lean thighs, squeezed cleavage, and parted lips when he heard *"What* . . . is she selling, lingerie or lap dances, and which one are *you* buying?"

He thought he recognized the voice.

"Hey, Jeannette! *Wassuuup?*" He gave the pretty girl a peck on the cheek. "What you doin' in my hood? Ain't you supposed to be up there in farm country?"

Farms were rare in the moneyed community where Jeannette Simpson attended private school. What *were* plentiful were stately homes, landscaped gardens, and American saddlebred horses. But the way Hustle saw it, if a place had grass, trees, and white people and it wasn't a city park, it was farm country.

"I wouldn't call it *that*," she said, laughing. "I just finished up my junior year, and I'm *so* glad to be back home for the summer. Even *projects* look good after a year of seeing nothing but green fields."

Like Hustle, she'd grown up poor in a watch-your-back kind of neighborhood where even young kids could tell the difference between the *crack* of fireworks and the *pop* of a handgun. Unlike Hustle, she worked hard in school and loved books, something she learned from her grandmother Anita "Nanna" Simpson, a high school teacher. When Nanna gave her a library card instead of "clothes money," as she'd requested, for her seventh birthday, Jeannette burst into tears. Ten years later there she stood, unapologetically unfashionable in nondescript jeans and a simple knit sport shirt.

It was well into the lunch hour, and the sidewalks were packed. Hustle wanted to invite Jeannette to grab a bite but had nothing in his pocket but a stolen chain, which wouldn't get them much food.

"So you out here shopping?" he asked, noticing her bag.

Jeannette was noticing something too. She liked his light eyes and soft features. But what was she *thinking*? Nanna would have cardiac arrest if she brought something *that* ghetto home.

"Yep. Books R U is having a 'Beach Reads' sale, so I got a few adventures, mysteries, romance . . . you know, fun stuff to take my mind off school."

Book and *fun* were not words Hustle put together in

the same thought. For him, *book* conjured up images of cops, fingerprints, and holding pens. And how could a book take your mind *off* school?

"Hey, if that's your thang . . ."

Reading was one of many *thangs* the two teens didn't have in common. A police car tore down Broadway, siren wailing.

"Uh, which way you headed, Jeannette? I'ma hafta get off this corner." He cut a nervous look in the direction of the squad car. Even when he wasn't doing anything wrong, he always felt like all police were after him. "People be bumpin' into you like it ain't nothin'."

"East," said Jeannette.

They headed towards Fifth Avenue, Jeannette talking books, Hustle talking rap music.

They had met that winter in a festively decorated classroom of Columbia College, the oldest college in New York State. Hustle's friend Nate was speaking at a holiday party for kids interested in learning about private schools like the one Nate attended. Hustle, fresh out of jail and a new probationer, showed up to surprise him.

Jeannette and Nate's girlfriend, Willa, also attended the school and had volunteered to help out. Jeannette and Hustle had danced together, and she liked him. But he was a little too boy-in-the-hood for her—the do-rag, the tilted baseball cap, the flowing T-shirt Nanna called a "Tskirt" . . . She wasn't even *trying* to feel that look anymore. How *gangsta* was it anyway when half the preppy boys in her school dressed the same way? The whole gangster-pimp-hoodlum thing was so negative. Nanna was right— "Boy in the hood today, boy in the wood tomorrow." Too many neighborhood boys ended up in pinewood coffins before they were even out of their twenties.

At Fifth and 46th, an African stood next to a row of pocketbooks laid out atop a cloth on the sidewalk. He motioned to Jeannette, pointing to his wares. Then he made the cultural blunder of pulling at her arm. "Come! Miss! Look!"

"Yo, man, you crazy?" yelled Hustle, grabbing him by the wrist.

The street vendor responded with an onslaught of insults in his native language, none of which, fortunately, Hustle understood.

"Man, I almost *lit* him up." They were crossing 47th Street. "Where these people come from anyway?"

Jeannette was more forgiving. "Oh, he just wanted a sale. This round-the-way girl from Brooklyn is pretty good at taking care of herself. I bet that's how they do it where he's from."

"Well, he need to get in his boat and row back or he gonna find out how we do it where *we* come from."

No, thought Jeannette, too much macho hood for her.

She changed the subject. "So anyway, tell me what you've been doing since the Columbia party."

"Time," he said, laughing. "Nah! You know I'm just messin' with you."

He searched for words that would portray him as being in the game, *any* game.

"You know how *I* roll," he said, lifting his cap and pulling it back on. "I'm into a few different things . . . some rap, some retail . . . Gotta get that *paper*, you know, cash money."

Jeannette's eyebrows shot up. "Retail? Isn't that what landed your re-*tail* behind bars in the first place?"

"That's a good one, Jeannette, you funny. I see you like jokes. You heard this one? What do a judge say to a innocent white defendant? 'Dismissed.' What he say to a innocent black man? 'Probation.' See what I'm sayin'? *That's* why I got probation. I was innocent as charged."

"Yeah, right, Hustle. You're about as innocent as O. J. Simpson."

"That's *real* cold. But hey, it's all hood. A little chill-out time on lockdown never hurt nobody. Take Marv'lous from Bed-Stuy. And Pranksta. The Trendy Crew. All them boys from the block done time. That's how we be keepin' it real, shorty."

She was annoyed.

"Uh-huh. Real *stupid*. And by the way, I have at least two inches on *you*. *Shorty*." She glanced at her watch. Her stomach was growling, her desk was piled high with work, and what was she doing wasting time with an aspiring inmate? She'd buy a sandwich on the way back and eat at her desk.

"Pranksta's a rich businessman whose record company probably *told* him to get busted so he'd get some street credibility since he *is* a bourgeois boy from the 'burbs."

"No he ain't. Pranksta took nine bullets in front of a nightspot over in—"

That was it. She *had* to call him out.

"*Hellooo!* His sister Melody goes to my school, and unlike me, she *ain't* on scholarship. They're straight outta Princeton, thank you. Anyway, even the real hoodies change up once they're rich. Marv'lous is about as from the block as J.Lo. And here's another scoop—girls aren't looking for guys with 'shot nine times' on their résumés." She walked faster, the distance between them growing. "I gotta get back to work, it's already after one."

"Work? I thought you was shopping. You got a gig over *here*?" asked Hustle, impressed by the location.

"At a publishing company. But I really have to run."

"You must got *mad* game. Hook a homey *up*!"

"They're not hiring. Anyway, summer jobs are for people who go to school in the fall, winter, and spring."

She ran up the block.

"Jeannette!" he shouted too late. "Can I get that number?"

5

HUSTLE HAD NEARLY MADE IT BACK TO THE SUBWAY
station when out of the blue thundered a sudden shower.
In seconds, everyone was dashing for cover. Hustle
ducked into the nearest doorway. The storm lashed the
giant pouting model, drenching her embroidered lace bra
and panties. The drumming rain lightened into rhythmic
tapping as it collected along ledges and dropped with a
tap . . . tap-tap onto the sidewalk. He pulled a pad from
his pocket and jotted down some lyrics.

> *She a hold-out shorty too nice to be naughty,*
> *seventeen not forty, lovin' school but she cool,*
> *both us be out da hood and she the one doin' good,*

but I brings da bling thing for her ice pinkie ring,
ain't gon' be no drop-off till I make it pop off.

"What you writing, your will?"

An old man, shielding his head under a soaked newspaper, had just ducked into the entryway.

"My ticket to some big . . . ass . . . bank, that's what."

"Is that a fact?" Faint sarcasm rang in the man's voice, like he too once had silly dreams. "Well, write one for me too, son. The good Lord knows I could use some of *both*." He shook with laughter, tickled by his own joke.

When the English scientist Charles Darwin hypothesized that Nature's preference for the strong assured only the survival of the fittest, never would he have imagined that a century later a black kid from Harlem would adopt the theory as his own personal creed. And yet, Hustle had done precisely that.

"I gets mine, you gets yours," he said. "*That's* the rule out here. Survival of the illest."

"If that's how your world works, then it'll be a mighty long time before my old ship comes in."

The nautical reference brought back images of Pimpsqueak and his concave chest and ship-patterned underwear.

"What's funny?" asked the man, seeing Hustle laughing.

"I'm laughing because I'm happy for you. Your ship just docked."

Like a magician about to dazzle his audience, he pulled ever so slowly from his pocket a beautifully crafted gold chain. The rain had stopped, and the yellow metal glinted in the sunlight.

"What you got here is a hundred percent solid gold, fourteen-karat. 'Cause you a cool dude, I'll let you have it for ninety. That's half off. You can't argue with a bargain like that, my man."

This man could.

"Even if I *had* ninety bucks—which I *don't*—I sure wouldn't waste it on no *pimp* chain. Black folk need to be gettin' *un*chained."

Hustle was a savvy street salesman and knew when someone was haggling for a better deal.

"I hear you. I'll take eighty."

"Boy, *get* out my face! I thought you had some *sense* under that hat."

Hustle dropped his treasure back in his pocket. He wasn't feelin' his groove and decided to go back uptown. At the subway, he squeezed past people climbing the stairs and descended into the vast station. His timing was perfect. A train was pulling in.

There were empty seats, but he chose to stand. People could start buck-wilding at any moment, and he felt better prepared for whatever broke out if he was on his feet. At 59th Street, professionals and executives rushed to meetings, at times colliding with a lagging tourist studying a subway map. Pickpockets waited patiently to seize upon that one moment of inattention their victims would regret for weeks. Police on heightened alert scrutinized eyes and faces in the hope that evil intent, if present, would show.

But terrorism was far from the minds of the pair who hopped into Hustle's car just as the doors were sliding shut. They were identically dressed, in pink sneakers with a frilly fringe, extra-low-cut hip-hugger jeans, and fitted tank tops with sequined lettering across the bosom. One read BROOKLYN and the other BABYGIRL. With every jolt of the train they slammed against each other, giggling and frantically grabbing on to the pole where Hustle was standing. One of those times he felt something like a cut and flinched.

"I am so *sorry*! My nails scratch you?"

Babygirl's gold fingernails extended far beyond her fingertips.

"Hell yeah, shorty. That's a personal injury."

But that cute face and hot little body, he thought, sure helped ease the pain.

"Just wish my shirt ain't been in the way, *heh heh*. So what's your name?"

"Shorty. Like you said."

The girls doubled over, holding their stomachs and screaming with laughter. Brooklyn began singing, "It started when we were younger and you were mine . . . my *Booooo*! You know you *love* him!" she yelled, shoving Babygirl his way. "You want him to *Usher* you down the aisle!"

As the train swayed, Hustle made a game of protectively catching the tottering girls, enjoying the sensation of their bodies crashing against his. They continued their mutual taunting.

When the train squealed into the next stop, out leapt the girls in the same way they'd boarded—seconds before the doors shut.

"Where y'all goin'?" called Hustle through the glass. "What's that phone number?"

They didn't even look back.

People read books and newspapers while others talked or just sat idly. Most had ignored the teenage flirt fest, a sight so common in the subway that it was routine. As long as the kids weren't bothering *them*, they didn't care *what* went on. What had gone on, however, wasn't any ordinary flirt.

"Dammit!" shouted Hustle, patting and feeling around in each pants pocket.

God*daaamn*. Gone. Jacked. By *shorties*.

He slumped onto a seat. Normally, he *never* let his guard down, no matter *where* he was. But who'd think a couple of cute . . . It wasn't like he ain't never rolled with some gold ropes or a stash of cash on him. He had . . . plenty of times. And he'd never had nothin' *that* wack go down. Feelings new to him, of anxiety and uncertainty, surfaced.

Resting his head against the window, he closed his eyes, rewinding and replaying the same scenes until he was certain he knew exactly when Babygirl had lifted the chain. Hustle may not have understood what had just happened, but Darwin would most likely have concluded that, once again, the illest had survived.

6

HARLEM USA WAS SPREAD ACROSS MORE THAN FIFTY CITY blocks. The famous neighborhood's past as a symbol of black cultural, political, and economic success was largely lost on Hustle, who knew it only as his personal purgatory of absent parents, dwindling funds, and a shaky future. Nor did he pay much attention to the new, booming Harlem of chain-store outlets, upscale shops, moneyed homesteaders, and, most famously, the offices of a former United States president.

Hustle's personal Harlem was sorely in need of a renaissance. For him, it was the place where a scared kid named Eric Samson had been ditched by druggy parents and dismissed by frustrated teachers. Home to a wretched child who was never given anything but *away*—first to relatives, then to neighbors. That boy, nicknamed Harlem Hustle, was now a perspiring teenager with a knot in his stomach.

His legs felt heavy as he walked, grimly reminiscing about the past couple of days. The store detective had thwarted him. Jeannette skipped without leaving a phone number. The old dude wouldn't buy the chain. Then those girls . . . He just couldn't get a break, he thought. He arrived at 128th Street, where he lived with a friend's family. That friend, Ride, was leaning against the stoop.

" 'Sup, H." They slapped hands. "Uh-oh, you got that head-knocking look. What happen?"

People lie for various reasons—to prevent a home visit from the guidance counselor (the hospitalized-parents lie), to sneak to a forbidden party (the study-group lie), to conceal a nocturnal eating binge (the I-don't-even-*like*-Oreos lie)—but Hustle's reason was one of the most powerful of all. He lied to save face.

"Ain't nothin'." He cracked his knuckles. "Some punks jacked me for a chain. They had to fight for it though. I was *doggin'* 'em, you know how I do—"

"Definitely," said Ride with admiration. "I seen you in action, like Demolition Man in the movies."

"—but they pulled the steel, so then I was like, *whoa*, here, it's yours. I wasn't takin' no lead for some fake gold chain."

Ride nodded his head. "You did right. A chain ain't nuthin' to be getting shot up over. How many was they?"

Hustle shrugged. He was sick of talking about it. "I don't know, three, two . . . a few. Big, inmate-lookin' steroid freaks."

Pointing his fingers like a gun, Ride said, "That's why I be *tellin'* you, don't leave home without the chrome. But you a hardhead."

Hustle's mood worsened.

"And you a *knothead*. What you think gon' happen if I get busted packin' heat while I'm on probation? My P.O. would have my butt on the Upstate Express in a flash." He lowered his voice. "I got rid of mine, and you need to lose yours too."

"Not me, I gots to keep protection, too many crazies out here. Anyway, a stint upstate ain't nothin' but a vacation from down here."

"What *you* know about it, like you ever done time! If jail sound so sweet to you, take *your* punk ass over to Rikers Island and parade it around. And make a video for me."

Fifteen-year-old Manley "Ride" Freeman was part irritating little brother, part best friend, and not necessarily in equal parts. Hustle let him join the Brotherhood, set up to keep drug dealers off their block, because of his imposing physique. In return, Ride had to get his parents to rent Hustle, who'd been living here, there, and everywhere, a room. Hustle managed a payment once every couple of months, then couldn't pay at all. The Freemans let him stay anyway. Whenever the Brotherhood needed wheels, Ride, known as GTA for "grand theft auto," was summoned. He could jump-start a "ride" as smoothly as if he'd turned a key in the ignition. The group disbanded after Hustle's friend Nate went away to school and the other two succumbed to violence and, ironically, drugs.

Hustle and Ride lived like brothers. And fought the same way.

"I got your video, Hustle, right here." Ride threw a flurry of punches, weaving and skipping back and forth.

"That's all you got, punk? You gon' last about five minutes on your vacation in jail!"

Their disputes, whether friendly or hostile, always came to blows. Ride usually won the boxing matches thanks to his crazy thrashing style, which made Hustle laugh so hard he couldn't fight.

"Oh, you want more, chump?" demanded Ride, punching wildly. "I got more, *lots* more!"

"You call that fightin'?" panted Hustle. "You sure you not wavin' for help?"

Neither saw a woman approach carrying a large grocery bag.

"Manley!"

Ride dropped his fists to his sides.

"Ma! I *told* you to call me Lee!"

"Boy, take this bag from me before I call you something worse. You better count your blessings that you even *have* a father to give you his name. Get inside and do your homework. I know it's not done. If you'd done it during the year, when you were supposed to, you wouldn't be in school right now while everybody else out having fun."

She narrowed her eyes at Hustle. "And what *you* laughing at, *Eric*?"

"Nothin', Moms, just Ride." He took the bag.

Lena Freeman shook her head. "Now give it to *him*," she said.

Hustle readily obliged. "Here ya go! I'm sure it ain't too heavy, you being so *manly* and all."

"Sucka," whispered Ride.

Mrs. Freeman unlocked the door to the small apartment, and they went inside.

In these times of nonstop television, hectic jobs, and single-parent homes, families rarely dine together, sharing stories over a meal, but the Freeman household was an exception. Dinner was a collective effort. If you didn't help, you didn't eat. The boys put away the groceries, tossing to each other packaged noodles and canned vegetables. Mrs.

Freeman added hot milk and butter to a pot of boiled potatoes and was mashing them with a fork. Manley Freeman, Sr., tugged at the kitchen table, which also served as the dinner table. The middle leaf extension clunked into place, then he cast above it a checkered cloth, which wafted down like a parachute. Once the meal was in place, they all sat down to dinner.

Mr. Freeman pointed to his bandaged wrist.

"Can you believe this?" he asked, managing to lift the heavy bowl of mashed potatoes. "That's what a crate of these potatoes will do if the forklift operator doesn't know what *he's* doing. The boss sent me home early."

He'd held all kinds of positions—fry and prep cook at a fast-food, janitor in an office building, parking garage attendant—whatever low-paid job a high school dropout could get. After a long stretch where high school graduates were squeezing him out of even *those* menial jobs, he finally found work doing warehouse inventory at a wholesale discount store.

"I still don't see why you can't collect some kind of disability, Man," said Mrs. Freeman. "Then you could stay home with me."

"Aw, it's not that bad. Plus, you know how these places are. Soon as a guy put in a claim, they find some reason to let him go." He shook his head like he'd seen it happen time and again. "Besides, baby, if I stay home with you, I'll end up *really* disabled."

"Go right ahead and be funny," she said, "but remember, I may *be* thirty-six but I don't *look* it, and many a man would *love* to spend his day with me."

Hustle and Ride lost it at the same time.

"Dis!"

"You gon' take that, Daddy?"

Mr. Freeman was unfazed. "After umpteen years of marriage, I ain't a bit worried." He placed his hand on his wife's. "I'd be the first one on line."

7

KNIVES AND FORKS CLINKED ON PLATES. MRS. FREEMAN noticed that Hustle seemed elsewhere. She'd never seen his father but knew his mother, Cat, from the neighborhood. A thin, jittery woman always asking for a loan. Then she vanished like a tip left on an unattended lunch counter. One day the poor kid would be staying with these folks, the next day with those. There'd been talk about Eric being involved in fights, shakedowns, stealing. When Manley joined that little block patrol group, she got to know Eric. Like any child thrown out on the streets to raise himself, he was angry and lost but mostly hurt. They gave him a roof over his head on condition that he keep his shady business outside. After his arrest, she kept a closer eye on him.

"And what'd you do today, Eric?"

"I was down at forty-deuce to meet this girl for lunch."

"I thought you're supposed to stay away from that area while you on probation," Mrs. Freeman said, glancing at her husband. If that boy thought for one minute he was fooling her, he had another thought coming.

"I know, I know. But I was in and out of there real fast."

Ride cut himself a slice of meat loaf. "Tell them about the time when those kids took you for that wanksta Furius."

Hustle kicked him under the table. He didn't want Mrs. Freeman to know he'd been in Times Square twice that week already.

"*What* . . . is a wanksta?" she asked.

"I thought you was hip, Ma. A *wack gangsta*. A fugazi . . . fake."

Mrs. Freeman wondered aloud why his vocabulary test scores were so low when he could remember nonsense like that. Ride's mind was elsewhere. He had a joke.

"Before you get going, I've got one for you," said Mrs. Freeman with irritation. She was worried. Ride had been a fairly average student up until high school, then just seemed to lose interest. He'd been left back a grade before and this year had been assigned to remedial summer school. She'd pretty much abandoned her dream that he might one day go to college.

"A black high school graduate has *less* of a chance of getting a job than a white *dropout*. And that's a *government* statistic. Look in today's paper, you'll see the article."

She eyed him triumphantly, as if the news would magically bring him to his senses. It didn't. Not because he didn't care, he did. He saw his father struggle to pay bills and knew his mother had college hopes for him. He wanted to succeed at *something*. It was just that there was no worse moment to bring up the serious topic of school than when Ride was already in joke mode.

"Then I should drop out now and bleach my skin white like Michael Jackson so I can get a job."

He cackled.

So did Hustle. "You a stone clown, man."

Mrs. Freeman agreed. "You hit the nail on the head, Eric. And at the rate he's going, he'll stay that way. Mark my words."

"Don't disrespect your mother," said Mr. Freeman.

"I was just playin'. I'm sorry, Ma, I know it's important. Can I tell my joke now?"

He drank some soda to clear his throat.

"How you know when a girl be from the projects?"

Project jokes were his favorites. Maybe they were poor, but at least they didn't live in the projects, where *really* poor people lived.

"When her first name start with Ta, La, or Sha."

Not one to stay angry very long and a jokester herself, Mrs. Freeman instantly perked up.

"That's good!" she said. "Here's one. How do you know when a *man* is from the projects?" She squinted teasingly at her husband, who had grown up in public housing.

"That's easy," he answered. "By his hardworking and responsible ways, right?"

"Wrong. He only goes to church on Easter, Mother's Day, and to meet women."

She had another one. "Why do project girls make bad pickpockets?"

Hustle started coughing. Mr. Freeman slapped him helpfully on the back.

"Their fingernails are longer than their fingers!"

Hustle turned impatiently to Ride. "Come on, finish your food. We don't got all day."

8

IT WAS A GOOD IDEA TO RUSH. BY THE TIME HUSTLE AND
Ride, both underage, flashed their fake IDs at the door of
the Crib, the club was already packed with a colorful mix
of young people from all over the city. No one dared challenge them as they pushed towards the front. The new hip-
hop club, located on the border of mostly black Harlem
and mainly white Morningside Heights, targeted rap music's most coveted converts—white kids with money.

It was Open Mic Night. Aspiring rappers took to the
stage to test their lyrics and beats, but mostly their nerve,
before a *very* live audience. The black male domination of
hip-hop was clearly *not* in effect in this venue, where the
mic was open to *anyone* with lyrics to spit.

"Y'all give it up foooor . . . *Suspence!*" shouted the emcee with a sweeping gesture of her hand. A white boy, defiantly preppy in a pale blue button-down shirt, slim-cut jeans, and dark blazer, strutted onto the stage to beats provided by his emcee, Machine, who was working the turntable in a tux. Perched on stools with identically crossed legs sat the Brain Dancers, brunette triplets, each reading a book.

All right, stop! collaborate and ha ha
I fooled you all with my Vanilla Ice blah blah.

Hoots greeted the name of the much-maligned first white rap star, who'd carved out his place in hip-hop history wrapped in an American flag.

The white rapper who burst onto the scene
And paved the way for my Suspence Machine
I'm Anglo-Saxon and a Protestant too
Or maybe Jewish, so what is it to you?

Cheers and applause. The preppies clearly outnumbered the homeys in *this* house.

No Hummers, mug shots, or tattoos on my *skin*
Why would I wear gold when that's what I invest in?

45

My blood is blue, and that I'll never let spill
My home alone is worth a multiple mill!

Suspence stopped, raised his fist in the air, and brought it down slowly to rest under his chin in imitation of the famous sculpture *The Thinker.*

Hustle was about to boo when a boom of applause and ringing whistles drowned him out. Ride leapt to his feet. "Y'all *craaaazy*! That shit wack! Come on, man." They stood and elbowed their way to the back of the club, where some girls wearing Barnard College T-shirts were debating the virtues of Vanilla Ice.

"You are *so* wrong about him. I mean, look how cute he is in that old 'Ice Ice Baby' video. Plus, he was a *totally* great dancer. And the hair, omigod, it was *tight*." Crystal paused, her blue eyes closing as she searched her memory for the latest Snoop-bonics. "He was off da hizzle, and that's *chuuuch fo shizzle, my nizzle*."

"Bzzzz," hissed Diamanté, as if shooing away an annoying insect. "Not."

"Look at *our* generation's white rapper, he totally hates girls, women, and bitches. And those are *his* words," said Krissa, snatching off her glasses. "I'm doing a paper on hip-hop misogyny but not just on the raps, I'm looking at the rap*pers* themselves. And it is *scary*. Dr. Dre once attacked a rap-show host, slammed her against a wall, chased her into the *women's* bathroom, grabbed her by the hair, and punched her some more. Did he ever hear of freedom of speech? That was in *Rolling Stone*. *The Washington Post* reported on the *many* domestic disturbance calls made to police from Damon Dash's Long Island mansion. And the woman who said he hit her is his kid's *mother*. And I *know* you remember Mystikal, who did 'Shake Ya Ass.' Well, he's shaking his in prison doing six years for sexual assault. I mean it, these guys are *truly* scary."

Ebonya shook a headful of dreadlocks. "Black women are already hoes to Snoop, bitches to 50 Cent, and every other kind of hole, dog, and freak to the rest of them. Then *white* Eminem gonna dis us too with trash talk like, and I quote, black girls are dumb."

Diamanté said she wished House of Pain would come back and make them all jump around again. "They were awesome. As for Eminem, like him or not, he's real. Vanilla Ice, fake. *Bzzzz*."

Ebonya dismissed them all with a hand wave. "Little of it is positive. There's Nas, there's the gay rapper Caushun, there's Erykah Badu, but she's more jazz than hip-hop. These commercial rappers are in it strictly for money. Do you think they care how much harm they do on their way to the bank? Not. I like *real* hip-hop. All this gangsta-ganja pop-hop is crap. I'm checking out the underground, listening to alternative sounds. Hell, I'd buy a Suspence record before giving *those* losers my money."

The others unanimously agreed on one point. Suspence? Now *that* was going too far.

A female voice blared over the mic.

"Can you *heeyah* me?"

"Yo, let's go, Hustle. I ain't stayin' for *this* wackness."

The wackness in question came with a mass of orange hair held up by a wide, dark green headband, a black GRUNGE LIVES T-shirt, shabby jeans with knee holes, and forlorn Army boots. The girl's saucy attitude rose to the challenge of the skeptical audience.

"Paulie C in the house, the white Missy Elliott! Same booty, different shade! Make some *noise*!"

Someone booed. "*That* enough noise?"

"Don't *hate* . . . *emulate*!" she responded, undaunted.

Ride had seen enough. "Let's bounce!" he said, standing to leave.

"Wait, hold up," said Hustle, grabbing Ride's arm and pulling him back down. "We *can't* miss this!"

A Linkin Park–like chant rose up from some front tables. "*You've* . . . become so dumb!"

She turned her back to the room, bouncing her ample attributes to the beat, then swirled to face off with the crowd.

The buck stops heeyah
the ice so deeyah

the gold hang neeyah
or split from heeyah,
champagne not beeyah
nice clothes to weeyah
or don't you deeyah
try to hit this heeyah.
if you hear me girls make ya mouth go Owww
if you feel me girls sing We want it now!

That first verse more than satisfied Hustle's curiosity. He nodded to Ride, and they shouldered their way out, Paulie C's voice at their backs.

Above, a full moon shone brightly. On the streets below, the atmosphere was electric with the energy of people roaming about in search of mirth or mischief.

Ride was incensed. "These days *any* kinda freak can be a emcee."

"You right, but you gotta admit, the *booty* was *bouncin'.*"

"Now on *that*, ain't *no* dispute."

They were almost across the street when Hustle spied Jeannette climbing into a cab with another girl.

"Wait here, I be right back!"

The other girl glimpsed Hustle running towards them. "Uh-oh. Homey Alert. Hurry up, get in!"

It was hard to tell who was more happily surprised, Hustle, who figured he'd blown it, or Jeannette, who'd regretted pretending she hadn't heard him asking for her phone number.

"Twice in one day?" said Hustle at the back window. "Girl, that *gotta* be about *somethin'*! You sure you live in the B.K., 'cause you steady hang in Manhattan."

"You're the one stalkin'! We got carded at the Crib—a friend from school was performing—so we went out to eat instead. Now I *am* headed to Brooklyn."

Their brief chat drained the cabdriver's patience. "Talk on street! Ride in taxi!"

Hustle poked his head in the front window. "You got a *problem*, Osama?"

"No more international incidents, Hustle." Jeannette hurriedly wrote her phone number on a scrap of paper. "We gotta go! Call me."

9

BOYS LOVE TO BOAST ABOUT EASY CONQUESTS. MALE peacocks parading the plumage of their jerseys, baggies, and hand-stitched sneakers, not just kissing and telling, possibly forgivable, but kissin' and dissin', a sin by any definition. Yet, they say nothing of the girl they yearn for, those scary, tender feelings concealed in silence.

Hustle dashed through the traffic, a big smile on his face.

"You hittin' that ho?" asked Ride, a leer in his voice.

The smile dropped. Hustle slammed him in the chest with his fist. "Shut up, she ain't no ho!"

It took Ride a few seconds to catch his breath. "What's *wrong* wichoo, Hustle? All damn *day* you been moody as a bitch with the curse, and I'm gettin' sick of it. You better take a pill or *something*."

He bopped to the corner. Hustle was cool money and all, but he always be taking stuff out on the same people he s'pose to be friends with. He blinked hard, wetting his eyelashes. He wasn't crying like no girl though.

Hustle followed him. "Yo, man, you know you my boy. We cool? Gimme a pound."

"You know I pays you no mind, chump," said Ride, giving him five.

Jeannette was not mentioned again.

They had no particular destination, that is, until one was presented to them in the form of a gold-roped entryway marked TUFF ROLLER'S VIP PARTY. One of the most successful rap labels in the industry was throwing a party not that far from Hustle's very own block.

"Yo, yo, yo," he said, elbowing Ride, "check it out."

Ride shifted emotional gears as quickly as his mother, and any trace of the feelings he'd had was gone. He was admiring a woman whose skimpy outfit displayed the rippled fruit of thousands of agonizing sit-ups and leg raises.

"I *am*, and she lookin' *real* good. How old you think she is? Maybe I can get a play."

"I ain't clockin' *her*. I'm talkin' about this *party*. It could jump *off* for me up in there. You know how many dope emcees signed up with Tuff Roller? Trendy Crew, Heist, Fort Hardknox, Pranksta, Slangstarr . . ."

Hustle breathed each name with reverence.

"Oh *man*, you right!" said Ride, reading the sign. "And we already on the celebrity carpet!" Beneath their feet lay a short strip of red carpeting. They slapped hands.

Hustle knocked at an imaginary door. "Knock, knock. Who's there? Red. Red who? Ready to *partaaay*. Let's do this."

The bouncer patted down a couple and waved them in. Hustle was next, Ride at his side.

The burly man surveyed them from head to toe. "This party's private. Very."

"It's all good, brother. I'm Double H and this MC Ride."

The bouncer checked the guest list. "Stop frontin'."

"Stop hatin'," said Ride, stepping forward.

"Hatin' on *what*?"

Guests were lining up behind them. The bouncer used his arm to try to steer Hustle and Ride away from the entrance.

"Later, playas, make some room, let the people in."

Ride pushed back. "Later for *you*, sucka. Get ya hands off me."

It was *on*. In the shoving match that broke out, the

bouncer grabbed Ride by the collar; Ride punched him in the face. Guests scattered, the women stumbling on high heels, the men hopping over the women. Some darted into nearby doorways that potentially held even greater dangers than a street fistfight. Hustle grabbed Ride and locked him in a bear hug.

"Chill, Ride, let it go!"

"That punk lucky I ain't strapped or he'd be spittin' lead!"

Ride flailed like a twisting cobra, raging to break from Hustle's grip. A detail of heavies surrounded them, gnashing their teeth and growling. The hired security was hungry to knock heads. Their boss ordered them to "stand down," military language the ex-Marine deemed appropriate to "civilian combat conditions" such as rap music events, gatherings combining New York cops and firefighters, and any place the Williams sisters wore their self-designed tennis outfits.

A teenage boy watching the altercation said a few words to the security chief, who ushered his men back inside the club. Hustle was trying to calm down Ride, who wanted to go home to "get something," when the boy approached and extended his hand.

"Spence Adams. You dudes were at the Crib earlier, in front, right?" He was wearing an elegant suit of white linen. "Suspence, remember? 'All right, stop! collaborate and ha ha.' What'd you think of the rap?"

54

"Wack," snarled Ride.

"Wrecked," said Hustle, shaking his hand. "But you stepping in on that bumrush, that was straight up cool. Thanks, man."

Spencer laughed. " 'Wack' and 'wrecked.' You two don't mince words, do you? I like goofing around on the open-mic rap scene. My dad owns Tuff Roller, that is, he owns the company that owns Tuff Roller. Come on in to the party, you're my special guests. What are your names?"

"Double H, a.k.a. Harlem Hustle!"

"Ride. I mean MC Ride!"

Like hip-hop superstars, they followed the red carpet into the players' ball, escorted by Spencer Adams, of Adams Global Electronics, parent company of an empire of subsidiaries, including BullsEye Liquors, owner of Tuff Roller Records.

The sound system was blasting Pranksta's hit "Bounce Da Bootay." Every rising rapper and hip-hop hanger-on was there, rocking diamond-studded crosses and white-gold chains. People greeted Spencer and his two friends with a smooth blend of false affection and phony deference.

"Sycophants," yelled Spencer over the music. "Suck-ups. Because of my dad!"

Hustle and Ride were too busy clockin' the fashion models dressed à la homegirl and grabbing hors d'oeuvres from the trays of white-jacketed waiters to hear their host. Spencer led them directly to the VIP room, where everybody was poppin' collars, doing the one-up thing. The star of *Panty Shield*, the hit comedy about a womanizing bodyguard, was shouting into his cell phone. Next to him sat the host of the popular game show *Birth This! Celebrity Mama Matchup*, who was bragging about his ratings. The Trendy Crew were sitting on a sofa, each with his arm draped around a girl in black shades. Hustle recognized a cutie with a curly, blond afro. It was the hip-hop queen PMS, who could spit righteously with the hardest male rappers. Throughout the night, whenever photographers snapped her photo, he made it his business to be right there.

Straddling a stool at the bar, Pranksta was talking intensely with an older man wearing a backward black Kangol. His graying hair was pulled into a ponytail. Everything Pranksta had on—cap, hoodie, jeans . . . even the sneakers—was from his own P-Soldier label. His face registered concern as he checked out the new jacks chilling with that nerdy Spencer Adams.

"Wassup, Spencer, my homeboy?" He grabbed his hand and shook it hard. "So who's your crew? You know I can't let the competition just slide by."

The introductions made, Pranksta began grilling Hustle on everything from where he recorded tracks to whether he had any television commercials. Hustle was deliberately vague, just to yank Pranksta's chain.

"We on a freelance tip right now, know what I'm sayin'? Tessing the waters to see who gon' take us to the bank."

Tony Motta smoothed his ponytail. A "consultant" at BullsEye Liquors and self-styled promoter in the music business, he was rumored to have ties to *real* gangsters.

"Lemme share some wisdom with you fellas," offered the promoter. "This grass may be greener, but it's crawling with freakin' snakes. Choose careful. Choose savvy. And stick with the kid," he said, mussing Spencer's hair. "He's got clout."

Pranksta fidgeted with his do-rag, as if it were hair. "Double H . . . Ride . . . welcome to the jungle, I mean, the business."

Spencer left his new friends to do their thing, preferring the company of his old ones. Hustle and Pranksta small-talked for a few minutes, then Hustle could no longer resist. He had to check Jeannette's claim.

"Yo, you got a sister name Melody at this school call Fletcher?"

Pranksta gave him a dirty look.

"Yes, I do. And don't even *trip* about her unless you want some mad *trife*. Have a good time, homeys, I got a show to do." He tapped Motta's shoulder. "You coming?"

Mad trife, mocked Hustle. If he *did* want trouble, Pranksta sure wasn't the one who'd scare him away from it.

While Pranksta performed "Flip Da Clip" from his gangsta rap album *Call to Harms*, Motta talked to Hustle and slipped him a business card. On the back it read, "Boom! Blowup time."

The party was still going on when they left on legs that felt rubbery from hours of dancing. The street out front was a showroom of double- and triple-parked Benzes, Hummers, Bentleys, a cherry red Karmann Ghia, and a customized SUV with twenty-four-inch chrome rims and double exhaust pipes. The sky was pink with morning as they eased quietly into the Freeman apartment.

There was no need for Lena Freeman to glance at the clock with the one eye she'd opened when she heard them creep in, as the room was lit with daylight. She did anyway. 5:24 a.m. She sucked her teeth, curled against her husband, and fell back asleep.

Hustle's body was tired, but sleep was not on his mind's agenda. Words freestyled through his head: *I love your raps, dude . . . Summer jobs are for people who go to school . . . Black folk need to be gettin' unchained . . . My nails scratch you? . . . You're my special guests . . . Welcome to the jungle . . . Boom!* When sleep came at last, he dreamed he was running through fields of exploding land mines. Every explosion sent high into the air flurries of hundred-dollar bills that snowed down like an avalanche until he could no longer see himself.

Parents have been known to mask in the name of discipline other, darker urges. Punishment, humiliation, even revenge. It's hard to know what inspired Mrs. Freeman to go through the apartment making noise soon after her husband left for work. She turned her Kirk Franklin CD up loud and kept the gospel rhythm with two pans.

"Everybody up! Rise and shine, boys! Nobody spends the whole day sleeping in *my* house!"

She burst into her son's room making a racket comparable to the steel drums of a West Indian Day Parade. "Manley!" Her next stop was the back room. "Eric!"

They dragged themselves to the kitchen and collapsed at the table, rubbing puffy eyes and scratching their heads.

"Maaaa," whined Ride, "we was sleep."

She hummed, stirring scrambled eggs with a wooden spatula. Hustle closed his eyes and, remembering, smiled to himself. Food, coffee, and a shower can revive a tired body, but nothing revives the soul like hope, and for once Hustle had it. He'd always measured his future by the close calls of his career as a petty criminal, not knowing when it, or he, would be cut short. Now he saw it stretched before him like a flaming red carpet. His life had done a front flip. Boom!

"Eric, it's getting towards the end of the month. Aren't you about due to see Miss Contreras?"

Yes he was, he said with a yawn. He'd go see his probation officer real soon.

Ride looked dazed. "It's eight o'clock, Ma, what you trynna do? Ain't no school on no Saturday."

"You boys gotta eat, and I can't be waiting around for you to wake up. Your mother got a world of things to do."

"Wassup widdat? Since when you be making us breakfast?"

Mrs. Freeman dished up the eggs, a faint smile on her lips.

They both crept back to bed as soon as Mrs. Freeman was gone.

10

THE FAMILY ROUTINE FOLLOWED ITS USUAL COURSE OVER the next weeks, with Mr. Freeman working, Mrs. Freeman running the home, Ride reluctantly dragging himself to school, and Hustle writing rhymes that came to him faster than his hand could capture them. But the memory of the Tuff Roller party remained fresh in Hustle's mind, pushing him, demanding that he make something happen. He knew he had good raps, but what he needed now was money, enough to put together a demo. It was time to sell off the last of his merchandise, which he and Ride had hidden away.

On summer weekends, entrepreneurial Harlemites short on cash take advantage of the busy streets and good weather to sell off their possessions. And no entrepreneur was as determined to make sales as the kid who'd once been called Harlem's professional shopper. He was sitting on a wooden crate making his pitch.

"Rest ya eyes on these bona fides, the best gear right here, recycled from downtown to uptown. Got the rags for your head and the sags for your hips. Sean Jean, Rocawear, FUBU, G-Unit . . . ain't name-droppin', just hip-hoppin', get your leisure-class clothes at underclass prices."

Girls held jeans to their hips, and guys pressed jerseys against their chests. He'd been at it all morning and had sold well.

"Got a vendor's license, young man?"

"Jeannette! You back on my stompin' ground again?" He hugged her, holding on.

"*All right*, Hustle," she said, pulling away. "It *is* weird how we keep running into each other, because I'm never in Harlem. Gotta do some research at the Schomburg for a school paper I'm getting a head start on." She looked at the clothes. "Where'd you get all this?" she asked with a tone of dread.

"Hey, don't say it like that, I already had them. I'm trying to get some money for a rap demo."

"Oh, the Fugazi rap thing."

Hustle burst out laughing. He couldn't have penned a better opening.

"Fugazi? You callin' *me* out as a fake? Yo, you don't

know me, you know *of* me. Or you soon will." He was having fun. "Check it out." He showed her the latest issue of *Rhyme Time* magazine. "Double H never slackin', always gettin' crackin'."

Jeannette's mouth opened, then closed. She'd just heard that PMS song "Gurlz on da Hoods" on the radio. And there was PMS herself with one arm around a little boy in a bandanna and baggies, and the other around Hustle! Jeannette read and reread the caption. "Rap sensation Pipdawg, hip-hop *divette* PMS, and newcomer Double H get their VIP chill on at Tuff Roller industry party. Insiders assured *Rhyme Time* that Pipdawg, who turned thirteen last week, drank only soda."

Hustle was stacking the clothes. He put them in a large shopping bag and left the crate where he'd found it.

"I gotta eat something," he said breezily, loving the expression on her face. "You hungry?"

11

"IT WAS THE MOST STRAIGHT UP *BOOYA* PARTY I EVER *been* at. Off tha hook, off tha chain, off everything. Totally dope."

Dunkin' Donuts was packed with people who looked like they could've used a good long fast. Hustle ordered honey-dipped doughnuts and orange soda, and Jeannette got a cream cheese bagel and milk. He insisted on paying.

With the excitement of a child on Christmas Eve who already hears the rip of wrapping paper and the whir of new toys, Hustle detailed what he ate, who he saw, the gear, the gold, the ice, the cars, how he and Ride were on the dance floor poppin' and lockin' all night. When he got to the part about Tony Motta, he looked around and lowered his voice.

"Tony knows A and R people, producers, radio DJs, everybody. He's the one who gets your music on the radio and TV. And the time I did on lockdown? He said it make me look good. Record companies be fighting over guys who still locked up. Since Pranksta's fallin' off—you was right, he *do* got a sister Melody and he *is* a chump—he lookin' for somebody new to step up to the mound. Maybe he be me. I'ma pull together a thousand bucks for a demo. Believe me, when it drop, it's gonna hit like a *rock*! But all this strictly on the down-low. Tony don't want no beef with Pranksta."

Jeannette was incredulous.

"But how'd you get in in the *first* place? I got turned away from the Crib, and that's nowhere *near* fabulous! Even *with* ID, don't you still have to be *invited* to those things?"

He told her about the red carpet fight. She dropped her bagel when Spencer's name came up.

"*Noooo*. Spence *Adams*? That's who we wanted to see at the Crib. He's Nate's friend! His father's in *music*? I thought his family was in electronics or computers or something."

She threw her head back, laughing. "I work for his aunt!" Hustle didn't miss the sexy slope of her neck.

"This is wild! It sounds too good to be true. These things don't *really* happen in real life."

"In the real life of Double H they do." He paused.

"And guess who my first rap about? *And it goes a little somethin' like this,*" he sang, then went into his rap, tapping beats on the table.

> *She a hold-out shorty too nice to be naughty,*
> *seventeen not forty, lovin' school but she cool.*

Hustle leaned back in his chair. "That's only the opening. Tony's feelin' it, but he want it more raw."

Jeannette felt flattered but played it off. Showing a boy your feelings right off the bat wasn't a good idea. She'd seen it go down like that with too many girls. A boy chases you for weeks, then as soon as he knows you like him too, all he wants to do is hit it and quit it.

"Well, sounds good to me. When you're onstage getting your Grammy and I'm in the last row of the top balcony, you better give the B.K. a big-up."

He promised. She had to get over to the library before it closed.

Jeannette hurried along Malcolm X Boulevard. Willa was probably checking her watch every two minutes and working up an eye-rolling attitude. Inside the Schomburg she greeted Mrs. Quilly, the old blue-haired librarian. Willa Matthews, wearing a Fletcher Furies lacrosse jersey and a baseball cap, was working at a computer console. She was the rather indulged only child of a well-to-do black Inwood family. Jeannette had less in common with Willa than with Hustle but they were each other's best friend at school.

"You're late," said Willa without turning around.

Jeannette sat down at the next console.

"I *know*, Will. Sorry. Remember Hustle? Nate's friend who we met at that Columbia thing. I ran into him selling clothes on 125th Street, the *third* time in—"

"Tacky," interrupted Willa. "And why am I *so* not surprised?"

She was positively allergic to anything ghetto. Even Harlem's own Chopin-playing, flaxen-haired, biracial, crossover R & B superstar Alicia Keys was starting to slip in Willa's estimation because of one too many "hoodlums" in the singer's videos.

"But listen, he's doing a rap demo, and he showed me a picture of himself in a magazine with Pipdawg and PMS."

Willa scrolled down the computer page.

"Pipdawg? PMS? Tackier. And why am I even more *so* not surprised?"

"You're really a trip, you know that?"

Willa could be *so* stuck up. Jeannette wasn't *even* trying to put herself through explaining anything to her. For the next hour and a half, they hopped on and off search engines, took notes, shared links, and collected information for their joint paper on the history of African-

Americans in Paris. Jeannette's focus was on legends like Josephine Baker, James Baldwin, Bricktop, and Richard Wright, while Willa was fascinated by the success stories of contemporary expatriate bankers and lawyers.

Twenty minutes before closing, Mrs. Quilly made her fabled announcement. "Researchers, scholars, and black folk of all ages! The library closes in precisely twenty minutes! That's twenty, people, not twenty-one."

The girls packed up and waited on the library steps. Judge Matthews was coming to pick up his daughter. He didn't want her in the Harlem subway.

Willa enthused about well-paid expats, French cuisine, opulent apartments, and European travel. Jeannette was impressed by the warm and seemingly color-blind welcome the French people extended to the early expats.

"From what I read, the French like black folks. Artists who were thwarted by American racism had a lot more freedom to express themselves once they arrived in France."

"Speaking of . . . ahem . . . artists, what's the real story with MC Hamm— I mean, MC Hustle? I didn't even know you two had kept in touch. *Please* don't say you're dating him."

"We *weren't* in touch," said Jeannette, feeling defensive. "I ran into him on my lunch break one day, then outside this club a few weeks ago, and then again today. All by coincidence."

"Omigod, you *are* dating him. What are you trying to prove, that you're still a project girl? He's a homeboy, Jeannette, h-o-o-d-l-u-m. You're not about that anymore, you're in a really good school now."

Jeannette sucked her teeth, rolled her eyes, wobbled her head, and deliberately did every other *homegirl* gesture in her repertoire. Willa couldn't be serious!

"How *you* gonna tell *me* what *I'm* about? Did your medication wear off or did you just not take it? Chill out, I'm *not* dating him. But I just might later. So! Your man's a homeboy from Harlem too."

Willa *begged* to differ. "Excuse me, but Nate attends the Fletcher School, okay? And he just bought a computer, not a beatbox."

"Yeah, well, Hustle will be rich and famous like Will Smith—who, by the way, rejected going to MIT to become the Fresh Prince—and we'll still be in our *really good school.*"

"Don't get me wrong, J, I like music too. *Good* music. India.Arie. Green Day. Ben Harper. And I *love* Tracy Chapman—she's awesome. Most rap is *by* and *for* people who think a plural is made with the letter *z*. And they're so violent they'd probably put a ghetto *fatwa* out on me just for saying that. These *homeboyzzz* think a hoodlum haiku about murdering people is going to make them rich. Ha! Ninety-nine percent of them fall right on their faces."

Jeannette *really* wished Mr. Matthews would show up.

"At least they're trying," she said. "And for your uppity information, I have all India.Arie's albums too. *And* Tracy Chapman's."

A black sedan turned onto the street and drove towards them.

"There's my dad! Let's not fight, Jeannette. I just don't want you getting mixed up with dead-end guys."

Jeannette waved hello to the judge, and Willa climbed into the back seat of the Lincoln Town Car. As it slowly pulled away from the curb, Willa stuck her head out the window. "My dad says they're called rappers because they have rap sheets a mile long!" Then she broke into song. "I'm *locked up* . . . they won't let me out . . . *locked up* . . . they won't let me out."

Jeannette tried hard not to laugh.

12

HUSTLE PASSED HIS DAYS WRITING LYRICS, COLLECTING beats, and dreaming about getting paid. Ride spent *his* in a hot classroom, taking make-up classes in reading and math, and railing against the injustice of it all. Jeannette's desk was piled so high with unsolicited submissions for her to log in that she didn't have a minute to think about anything else.

The day Hustle picked up the demo of "Back-Seat Shorty" from Uptown Digital recording studios, his spirit was as buoyant as his wallet was light. Hustle bounded into the apartment and found Ride watching television and doing his fractions homework. He grabbed Ride's arm, led him to his room, and nearly slammed him down on the mattress.

Ride coughed, waving his hands in front of his face. "Whatda . . . ? You ain't beat the dust off this thing *yet*?"

"I *did*. Now stop *crying*. Stay still and the dust will too." He held up the CD. "I got the verse. Tony changed a few things, and I *killed* it in the studio."

Hustle placed the CD in the player and pressed Play. Backed up by a thumping beat, a strong bass, and an old-school sample from "Super Freak," Hustle's deep voice held a natural street flava:

She a back-seat shorty, know how to be naughty
bust her out she cry Lawdee
bust her out she want more-dee
for some booze and that stem, she let you slide right in
and even taste her friend, while she do your friend Ben
bust her out she cry Lawdee
bust her out she want more-dee
booty outta control, watch it bounce and then roll
it even bend the rim, on my Mercedes-Benz.

Ride punched the mattress, releasing a mushroom cloud of dust. "That's some ill *shit*! The beat be dope, the hook on fire, the rhyme flow . . . You gon' destroy 'em!"

"Boom," said Hustle with quiet confidence, "we gonna *do* this thing."

They hugged, laughing and coughing. Hustle made it

to the post office just before closing and mailed the demo to Tony Motta. That evening Hustle phoned Jeannette and asked her out. This weekend wouldn't work, she said, but next weekend, sure, she'd like to check out a movie.

He left home on a Saturday afternoon immaculate in a powder blue warm-up suit with white sneakers, a white nylon do-rag, and a blue cap. He boarded a subway train bound for Sheepshead Bay, Brooklyn.

Superstitious souls might conjure a connection between Sheepshead Bay's significant crime rate and the fact that the neighborhood takes its name from a "convict," the alias given to the sheepshead fish because its stripes resemble prison stripes. The large fish was a staple for Sheepshead Bay's earliest settlers, the Lenni Lenape Indians, living contentedly in their little village. Then, in the blink of an eye, there went the neighborhood as first Dutch, then English, settlers flooded in.

The projects themselves, Sheepshead Bay Houses, were built in the fifties for white, middle-class residents who'd disappeared from sight by the time a couple thousand poor, black people had moved in some twenty years later. The area's newest arrivals were mostly Russian and Asian, along with a few African immigrants. They all knew of the projects but rarely, if ever, ventured inside. Hustle waved to one of them.

"Miss! Which way the projects?"

The colorfully dressed woman, bouncing a baby strapped to her back, fled to the other side of the avenue.

"Yo, lady! Where you goin'?"

Hustle entered a grocery store. The man at the counter greeted him with a blank look.

"Where the projects at?"

"Nie rozumiem."

They stared at each other. Hustle asked again, louder.

"Nie rozumiem," responded the store owner.

"Come on, dude, speak English. Projects? Sheepshead Bay?"

Recognizing the word, the Polish immigrant's face brightened.

"Yes! Shee-bed! Yes!" He showed Hustle three fingers, then pointed at the street. *"Trzy blokuje zachód!"*

Hustle was relieved they'd managed to communicate and offered his hand. "Thanks, homey, gimme five."

The store owner slapped his hand on Hustle's, grinning widely. Just as he'd said, three blocks down stood Sheepshead Bay Houses, a complex of six-story red-brick buildings. He located Jeannette's and rang at Apartment 5-A. She opened the door, wearing a yellow short-sleeved blouse that looked new and jeans that were freshly ironed.

"Hey. You found it."

"Ain't *no* borough a mystery to me."

He stepped towards her. "Don't just stand there, gimme some love."

She stepped back. Nanna would *not* be pleased to catch them kissing.

She directed him to the living room. "My grandmother's waiting to meet you."

Grandmother. The word evoked in his mind images of a plump, blue-haired biddy in standard old lady wear—a flowered housecoat and fuzzy house shoes. Not surprisingly, he was unable to disguise his reaction to the handsome woman in the white, fitted top and black slacks. This grandmother had model good looks and the height to go with them.

"*Goddaaamn*, you a *grandma?*"

Jeannette punched his arm. "Hustle!"

"Yo, you gotta admit—"

Another punch shut him up.

Mrs. Simpson would be the last to admit it, but with the big *five-zero* just a blink away, she was increasingly open to flattery from any source, even from what she saw standing before her—a hoodlumish looking teenager who probably didn't have a pot to pee in.

"I'll take that as a compliment. Nice meeting you too. Jeannette seems quite taken with—"

"Nanna!" exclaimed Jeannette, silencing that line of talk as well.

13

THE COFFEE TABLE WAS COVERED WITH PLASTIC PLATES of dill pickles and cucumbers, spicy chicken wings, and cold cuts, and Hustle took full advantage of the free food. Mrs. Simpson watched him with a growing sentiment of disapproval that had little to do with Hustle and everything to do with another young man who years ago had sat on her couch stuffing himself. Jeannette's father, whose name didn't merit remembering.

She'd taught teens at the local school for many years and believed that education was not *a* path to a full and successful life—it was the *only* path. It was a terrible blow when her own daughter, Dalia, had a baby before graduating high school, then vanished with her loser of a boyfriend. Look at that getup, she thought, eyeing Hustle's do-rag and cap, the warm-up suit, the pricey sneakers. She'd seen scores of them over the years, dropping in on classes like visiting tourists and dropping out before she even knew their names. Clones. These boys might as well be wearing maintenance men uniforms, she thought, the only jobs any of them would ever get. *If* they were lucky. The child Dalia left behind had grown into an intelligent young woman full of promise. Nothing and no one was going to jeopardize that promise.

Safe conversation explored the weather, the new cheesecake menu at Junior's Restaurant, the lack of jobs for young people. This last topic segued into less safe territory.

"So, Hustle, I hear you're a rapper?"

"Uh-huh," began Hustle. "I'm about to drop a little sumpin' on 'em." He took a gulp of grape soda.

Mrs. Simpson had strong views about rap music, which Jeannette had made her promise not to share.

"So what are your raps . . . about?" Mrs. Simpson inquired, a faint rebuke in her "about." "Is there some kind of message, or is it the same ol' "—she felt Jeannette nudge her—"songs?"

"I wrote one about this girl I like."

Jeannette groaned. She hoped it wasn't an embarrassing love song.

"I'd love to hear it," said Mrs. Simpson drily.

He faced one of those risky moments in life where

vanity and caution collide. The need to front and the wish to chill lock in struggle like a pair of champion wrestlers. His loud ego pressed him to show off, pop some collar. A small voice told him to just be cool. A small voice he ignored. He remembered Motta's changes and felt a twinge of discomfort. He ignored that too.

He made some beatbox sounds into his hand and said, "After that part, I spit my rhymes."

"Not on me, I hope."

Jeannette nervously suggested they get going if they were gonna make the movie.

"No, wait, you have time," said Mrs. Simpson. "I want to hear this."

Bobbing his head, Hustle let loose.

She a back-seat shorty, know how to be naughty

A sensation of heat spread from Mrs. Simpson's body to her face, accompanied by faint dizziness.

bust her out she cry Lawdee
bust her out she want more-dee—

A sudden contraction of the muscles connected to her hair follicles caused the hairs on the back of her neck to stand up.

for some booze and that stem, she let you slide right in.

She swung her fierce gaze from Jeannette, who wouldn't meet it, to Hustle. "That's *enough. More* than enough. In fact, that was far too much."

Hustle neither saw the darkening sky nor felt the first droplets of the approaching storm. "Hold up, Nanna, you can't really feel the flow without the phat beats and special noises. Then we drop a sample of 'Super Freak' . . ."

Mrs. Simpson was livid. She jumped to her feet and spoke in the chastising tone of an outraged teacher to an insulting student. "*Super Freak?* Listen to me, young man. First of all, my *name* is Mrs. Simpson. Secondly, Jeannette is no back-seat shorty that you, or anybody else, is going to be sliding in. And when she *does* find a young man to settle down with, I expect her to bring in-laws to my home, not outlaws."

Jeannette searched for words that would smooth things over but found none. What, after all, could she say? Nanna didn't just *dislike* Hustle, she *hated* him. And right then, Jeannette felt like she hated him too. *A back-seat shorty know how to be naughty.* What happened to her being nice, not naughty? *Bust her out she cry Lawdee.* That was just plain stupid.

A lightbulb went off in his head, writing appeared on the wall, and, at last, Hustle picked up the clue phone. He realized he'd messed up. "Don't take it like that, Na— Mrs. Simpson. Them lyrics ain't—"

She stamped her feet so hard both Hustle and Jeannette winced. "I'm *talking*! You call that filth *lyrics*? Describing black girls like they're pieces of meat is not *phat*. Calling yourselves pimps, gorillas, and dogs is not *dope*. Bragging about killing folks is not *fresh*."

"I don't—"

"Let me *finish*. This whole rap so-called culture is nothing but a money machine feeding on woman-hate and the worst stereotypes about black men. Can't you see that? A handful of black rappers and a helluva lot of white businessmen are getting rich at the expense of our children, who could be getting an education if the people they look up to told them it meant something. Instead, they're strung out on some drug they copped from some wannabe rapper needing cash to make a record."

"I would never—"

"Interrupt me again!" she threatened. "And I'm supposed to see these *vultures* as heroes? Because they donate a few dollars to a crack baby charity when *they* sold it to the mother in the *first* place? You know what I see? Pushers flaunting and wasting their money, living *alone* in some ridiculous twenty-bedroom mansion when people are sleeping on the *streets*, parading around with the seat of their pants sagging low as a baby's shit-filled diaper!"

"Nanna!" cried Jeannette.

Mrs. Simpson fell silent. Hustle tugged at his do-rag. Jeannette fumbled with her beaded bracelet. A clock ticked. Minutes dragged by like molasses. Then Hustle said simply, "You right."

Mrs. Simpson sat down. Jeannette exhaled.

"But I ain't made this world, and I ain't here to save it. I'm on my own, I got *nothin'*. No family, no schoolin', no skills . . . zip. Who's savin' *me*? This probably my one shot, the one chance I might ever get in this messed up life."

Jeannette looked glumly at her watch. It was too late for the movie.

Strong emotion and spicy food make a toxic mix. Hustle asked for the bathroom. As soon as she heard the door latch click into place, Jeannette spoke up. "I can't believe you *went* there, Nanna."

"Sweetie, that boy's just a—"

"You *promised*."

The women talked quietly. The one detailed Hustle's glaring flaws and bleak prospects. The other protested and pleaded. Mrs. Simpson was firm. *No*, she didn't hate the boy, *yes*, she would try to be a little nicer, but *never* would she apologize for speaking her mind. Jeannette complained that she'd made so little effort, *none* really. She'd taken one look at Hustle and decided he wouldn't do.

"Yet *you're* the one always saying people shouldn't judge a book by its cover."

"Well *that* book," said Mrs. Simpson, nodding her head towards the bathroom, "I've already read."

The latch clicked again. Jeannette gave her grandmother an imploring look. Mrs. Simpson shrugged, a sign that might have signified an indifferent *whatever*, a hostile *get over it*, or a supportive *don't worry*.

Hustle opted for a chair instead of the couch. As he sat down, the plastic cover made a low squelching sound. He laughed stiffly. "Don't think *I* . . ." His sentence trailed off into an uncomfortable smile.

I got nothin'. No family, no schoolin', no skills . . . zip. His words hung in the air like sad shadows, darkening the room. Pitiful. It wasn't that she didn't feel for him. She just wished Jeannette would meet a nice boy with promise up at that private school. When Dalia got messed up with that no-good . . .

Jeannette announced that the four o'clock movie they were supposed to go to had started. In response, and much to her granddaughter's surprise, Nanna made an offer. They could watch a film in her room. She had loads of movies and documentaries, she said. And more than a little bit of guilt about how she'd talked to Hustle, as if the bad in rap music were his fault. But this, she didn't say.

"I could whip up something for dinner, or Jeannette

could make popcorn. A stack *that* high of schoolwork's waiting for me in my office, so the room's all yours." As if thinking aloud, she addressed Hustle without looking at him. "I even have some rap DVDs: KRS-One, Queen Latifah, MC Lyte, De La Soul. Golden oldies, but they're good."

If Hustle liked or even recognized the names of those old-school progressive hip-hop artists, it didn't show in his faint nod. He was mentally rewriting "Back-Seat Shorty." In contrast, Jeannette's feelings radiated. She and Nanna often watched movies together, but the room had always been strictly off-limits to *all* Jeannette's friends, male *and* female.

"Thanks, Nanna!" she sang. "I'll make popcorn."

The popcorn settled Hustle's stomach, and *Love & Basketball* lifted his spirits. Maybe too much. He tried to make his move during the movie. The hand casually resting on Jeannette's shoulder brushed her chest.

"Don't even *think* about going there. My cookies stay in the jar . . . with Ciara's."

He played it off like it was an accident. They watched a second movie, *Guess Who,* and the evening was over.

The ride home seemed extra long. With 50 Cent's "Candy Shop" beat in his head, he wrote some new lyrics in his pad:

This shorty make me wanna stop
my hoodlum ways and reach the top
but movin' gear be all I got
don't wanna hafta end up shot . . . whoa.

The subway rumbled through tunnels and rattled over bridges. And Hustle wrote, all the way to Harlem.

14

IT SOUNDS TOO GOOD TO BE TRUE. **THAT WAS JEANNETTE'S** reaction to Hustle's tale about the Tuff Roller party and Hustle's serendipitous encounter with Tony Motta. She was right. The truth is, something that seems too good to be true is usually neither good nor true.

It seemed to Hustle that it had been ages since he'd sent the promoter his demo. And still, no response, no feedback, nothing. What was the hang-up? He could never get the man on his office phone, and calls to his cell went directly to voice mail.

Hustle was losing patience. "He must have the demo by now. Plus, I sent him some new lyrics for 'Back-Seat Shorty,' " he complained to Ride. "Maybe he not feeling it so he ducking me."

Sitting on the back of a park bench, they watched indifferently as the streetballers on the basketball court repeatedly fouled and cursed each other. The drone of Riverside Drive traffic blended with sounds of dogs barking and children playing. A gray-skinned stick of a man with weird, sparky energy bounded up to them. He stared expectantly at Hustle, then asked, "Yo, Money, you straight?"

Hustle kicked at him as he would a dog, just missing the man's bony hip. "Back up, man, get outta here! I ain't no drug dealer!"

"Them fiends *steady* be sweatin' you," said Ride, throwing a kick too as the addict made a speedy retreat. "You must got that slangin' look."

"If this rap thing don't hit . . ." Hustle left it at that. Of course, he'd never go there, but sometimes when he saw all the stuff the drug dealers had and all the stuff he didn't . . .

Ride gave a loud clap. He had an idea. A musical one.

"Check it out, why don't you G it up, put some gangsta stuff in there, like, you cruisin' in your ride, right? Strapped. Then you see them dudes who jacked you for your chain, so you creep to a slow speed, then you drop 'em. You know how we do."

He nodded his head, agreeing with himself. In that, he was alone.

Hustle's shove dumped Ride onto the grass. "What

you talkin' about, how *we* do? How *who* do? I ain't no gangsta, and I ain't trying to write no wack Cali drive-by bullshit. It *spose* to be a LL Cool J kinda *love* song for the ladies!" He hopped off the bench. "Yo, let's jet. Ain't nobody got no game out here. A grandmomma could sink more baskets than these clowns."

They wandered streets crammed with storefront churches, doughnut shops, clothing outlets, hair salons, soul food restaurants, and liquor stores. On Frederick Douglass Boulevard they saw a long line of people outside the Hue-Man Bookstore. A window poster advertised a memoir reading by an African-American expatriate. Ride stopped to read it.

"Why a girl from the projects gon' go live all the way in some foreign-ass country like Paris when we got everything right here in America?" He was truly puzzled.

"To get away from *your* wackness." Ride's stupid suggestion that he make his song about killing was still bugging him. "How you gonna say we got everything when *you* ain't got squat?"

Tall black locust and ginkgo trees shaded their walk along Adam Clayton Powell Boulevard. At Central Park, hundreds of acres of woodlands, lawns, and water lay before them. The casual and constant pace, the sun, and the fragrant air conspired to lighten Hustle's mood.

At the Harlem Meer, men fished and swans floated. The boys unknowingly passed through what was once Seneca Village, a part of the park that had been a nineteenth-century community of more than two hundred African-American property owners. It was razed in 1857 to allow for the creation of Central Park. But on that gorgeous summer day, urban history was as far from everyone's mind as a hot comb from a Rastafarian's locks.

They arrived at a meadow where sheep once actually grazed. Spread over fifteen acres of grass and bordered by oaks, elms, maples, and plane trees, Sheep Meadow was the perfect spot for them to rest after their long urban hike. Barefoot girls and shirtless boys shot whirling Frisbees over the heads of sunbathers, book lovers, and picnickers. A panoramic view of soaring residential towers formed part of a band of luxury buildings that encircled the park like a magnificent ring.

"*Look* at that." Hustle was squinting at the San Remo building's twin twenty-seven-story towers, each topped by a circular temple.

"You can have them haunted temples of doom. I like the funky crib over there." Ride pointed to the Art Deco–style Century Apartments.

"*You* funky, son, put your arm down."

Ride tried to grab him, but Hustle was too quick. At Columbus Circle, a cop took mental note of two young blacks running from the park. An arm-in-arm couple reflexively pulled closer together. The vendor inside a small newspaper stand watched their arrival with a sense of dread.

"Hey mister, you got Jawbreakers with the bubble gum inside, the big ones?" Ride studied the rows of candy.

The man handed him a box. "Sebenny-fie."

"Seventy-five cents? They *fitty* cent uptown."

"Sebenny-fie."

Ride felt around in his pockets, talking to himself. "Ain't that a trip, seventy-five cents for some stale Jawbreakers. I can get *two* packs of Jawcrunchers right near my school for *that* much, and they the same thing."

He looked at Hustle.

"Nope."

"Don't be like that, lemme get a quarter. You know I'm good for it."

"Nope."

"Come on, *Hustle*." A faint whine slipped into his voice.

"Here!" Hustle tossed a quarter at him. "Why you fiendin' for candy anyway, like a little kid? And you better pay me back!"

Grinning *exactly* like a little kid, Ride tore open the box and popped two in his mouth. A thought flashed in Hustle's mind as they walked down Central Park South eating candy.

"I'm gonna pay him a little visit, that's what I'ma do!" He read the business card in his hand. "He don't stay too far from here."

Ride wanted to go, but Hustle said no. *He* was the one Tony Motta was doing business with.

15

HUSTLE DIDN'T NOTICE THE FURTIVE GLANCES AND QUICK-
ened steps that met him as he strode up Park Avenue in
his brown hoodie and double-knit black pants with beige
side trimmings. He hesitated outside Motta's residence.
Maybe misgiving slowed his course. Or perhaps cold feet.
Or simply fatigue.

A uniformed doorman pulled open the glass door,
heavy with wrought-iron work. The entrance was ornate
and the lobby quiet.

"You here for Tony Motta?" inquired the man, knowing the answer. Mr. Motta's clients were easily recogniza-
ble. He lifted the intercom receiver. "What's the name?"
He announced, "Mr. Hustle."

The elevator's lighted buttons tracked Hustle's ascent, and a loud *ping!* announced his arrival at Penthouse Level. He entered a gleaming apartment of mirrored halls and ceiling chandeliers. Wall-length windows with sliding doors opened onto a wraparound balcony. The furniture was white and the walls adorned with music industry plaques and framed photos of Tony Motta beside hip-hop artists, TV personalities, and local politicians. The full bar was stocked exclusively with BullsEye brand liquor.

Hustle didn't expect to run into Pranksta.

"Hey, man. Wassup, Money?"

Pranksta gave him a big smile. " 'Sup, playa? It's all good, gots to be, dawg, gots to be. Would love to hang, but you know how it is . . . business, business, business. Tone's in his office."

Pranksta had on regular slacks and a red pin-striped shirt. Hustle thought about how he'd be taking Pranksta's spotlight, but hey, that was the game. And *he* was the new playa.

Motta had watched the encounter on a small closed-circuit screen.

"Back here, Hustle, the office on the right!"

Cigar smoke clouded the air. The man looked much older without his hip cap. A strip of gray, crinkly hair fringed the bald pate of his head.

"Sorry to just drop in, Tone, but I was over at the park and figured . . ."

"Hey, we're all family, am I right? Have a seat before you wear out your sneakers. Me and Pranksta were just discussing some business and your name came up."

His cell phone rang.

"Uh-huh . . . hmmm. You done? Okay, now read my lips, I got it in writing, you son-of-a— Oh really? I'll have you *and* your disbarred lawyer in a rathole so fast— Sue *this*, you stinking piece of crap."

He closed the phone and slipped it in the breast pocket of his charcoal gray, single-breasted suit. "A *pain* of a business associate . . . fuggedaboutit. So how you been, my friend?" .

The telephone conversation had impressed Hustle. Tone was the kind of dude he was glad to have on *his* side. He shifted his weight in the comfortable chair. It was almost unreal, but here he was, sitting in a promoter's office, about to get *his*.

"I been all right. Getting, you know, kinda *itchy* about the demo, *heh heh*. You had a chance to pass it on to the Tuff Roller people? I hope you got the new 'Back-Seat Shorty,' I put it in the mail about two—"

Motta puffed on his cigar, his cheeks filling and emptying. "It's been a freakin' zoo around here, deals, fights, phones, pagers. When I retire I'm going to buy me an island and go live on it. What you just heard, I go through the same nonsense ten times a day. I don't know what's wrong with people, they make a deal then they want out . . ."

Hustle shook his head to show he shared Motta's disgust with people like that.

"But anyways, getting back to the rap . . . you did a good job. It's more radio-friendly but hasn't lost that street edge."

Hustle was thrilled. "I gave it a softer flava, you know, for the ladies!"

"I intend to push for heavy airplay, and I mean *saturation*. Of course, nothing's free, it'll cost me, but that's the business. And I've locked up a solid video rotation deal . . ."

Hustle almost gasped. He was doing a video!

"You the *man*, Tone, and that's for *real*!"

Motta slid a sheet of paper towards him.

"So here's where *you* come in. This little note just says we wrote the rap together, you agree that full copyright ownership—don't worry about the legalese—be in the name of Archibald Bidon, that's Pranksta, and we've paid you a hundred dollars. That's a lotta dough for a rap from an unknown. I'll have to do some arm-twisting at Tuff Roller, but I'll get it. Here, use my pen." He turned the fountain pen between his fingers. "Look at this thing—

it's an Aurora St. Petersburg, Limited Edition. A seven-hundred-buck ink pen. A good old-fashioned Bic would do me fine, but in this crazy business you gotta impress, am I right?"

Hustle looked at the pen. He looked at the note. Something was wrong. No, something was *wack*.

"Wait, wait a minute, I'm not following this too good. What Pranksta got to do with it? *I'm* ready to do this thing. When I go in the studio? And what about the video? Don't I need to be . . . I don't know . . . *doing* something for that, rehearsing?"

"Uh-oh. Sounds like we got ourselves a little misunderstanding here. Pranksta's been in and out of the studio—he's recorded it already. We're talking to different directors for the video. Lemme tell you why Archie needs your help, Hustle. He's a good kid, he's got the right look, can talk the talk and walk the walk, but first problem, he's from upper-middle-class Princeton. Second problem, now he's a millionaire. How's he gonna do 'street hood' when he's never even *been* in the hood? The only street he's interested in is Wall Street. The only thing *gangsta* about Mr. Bidon is his gangster action figure doll."

He puffed on his cigar. "Listen, I know how you feel, you're young, you're hungry—"

Hustle banged his fist on the desk. "Damn *right*, I'm hungry. *I* wrote them rhymes. Those lyrics is Double H *dope* and ain't nobody rippin' me off for 'em. Bump the record deal, I'll go independent. Y'all want my rhymes and beats? Then gimme a grand or you can go suck on your fancy pen."

The cell rang again. Motta shut it off. He adjusted the knot of his handmade silk tie.

"You want a thousand dollars?" He rose. "Come here, my friend, lemme show you something."

He walked Hustle towards the sliding glass doors. Hustle stopped halfway.

"Jeez, don't be scared. I'm a businessman, not a street thug. You gotta see this view."

They stood on the balcony. From the street far below, traffic noises floated, soft and distant.

"Ever hear of Menudo? You're probably too young. A marketing whiz packaged five cutesy Puerto Rican teeny-boppers into a singing group—Ricky Martin was one of them—taught 'em some songs, a few moves, and set 'em loose on the girls. Boom! They exploded onto the scene and ruled the eighties. But the catch was that they had to stay teenage forever. So soon as one of the boys' voices dropped or he got a little facial hair, they rotated him out. The Revolving Menudos," he said, laughing, "that's what we called them. Kids revolved in and out of the group like on an assembly line."

Hustle felt pressure on his arm. Motta was pushing him against the railing.

"What you *doin'*, *man*?"

"That's you and all your rapping *homeys*. Rotating chumps on gold chains. Generic. You should learn that word. And *who* holds the end of that chain?" He used his powerful upper body to put even more weight against Hustle, bending him backward over the railing.

"*I* do, kid. *Men* like me. You think some diamonds in your belt buckle, your name stitched on the ass of a pair of dungarees, your own record label makes you powerful? *We* run the corporations that *own* yours, and you do nothing unless *we* green-light it. That's how America works, buddy, one guy owns the next guy, right on down the chain."

His hands gripped Hustle's shoulders. "You know why white men can't jump? Because we don't *have* to. We tell *you* bozos to jump, and you say, 'How high?' "

Hustle could barely breathe. He was bent over the railing and his back hurt. Wind rushed in his ears.

"What *don't* you understand about 'jump'? *Do it!*"

"Aight! *Keep* it, man, you can *have* it. I don't want nothin'!"

Motta smacked him in the face. Hustle spun away, his do-rag catching on the tip of a wrought-iron leaf. He stumbled to a chair, gasping.

"You choking, *dawg*? You trembling like a girl? *So* sorry. My fault. My bad."

He crossed out the payment amount and shoved the contract in front of Hustle, which the teen signed.

"Now get the hell out my sight! And if you go shootin' your freakin' mouth off, I know how to shut it."

Hustle stumbled to the front door.

"Yo!" called Motta sarcastically, waving a thin cloth. "You forgot your scarf!"

Hustle didn't stop running until he was inside Grand Central Terminal, safe among the commuters. He found a quiet corner and slumped onto the floor beneath the station's starry ceiling.

16

BLACK BOOTS STOPPED IN FRONT OF HIM. THERE WAS
little chance of mistaking the dark green and black combat uniform. And absolutely none of not recognizing the
long, black barrel of a U.S. Army–issue automatic rifle.

"Let's go, kid, I'm gonna have to ask you to move
along. You can't sit here. Security."

The city's public transportation system, bridges, and
tunnels were on heightened alert. Most New Yorkers were
unfazed, having grown used to their city being the wet
dream of desperate zealots. Residents went about their
business, but those protecting them were tense. The Na-
tional Guardsman, who a few months earlier had been
counseling juvenile offenders, stuck out his hand. Hustle
let the soldier help him to his feet.

"I'm okay," he said, hurriedly wiping his runny nose and wet eyes. "Kick butt, dude."

The serviceman gave a thumbs-up and continued his patrol.

Mr. Freeman was reading the newspaper, and Ride was reluctantly doing homework. A key was jiggling in the lock.

"Lee, go let him in. I keep meaning to get that lock replaced."

Ride bolted to the door. "Yo, H, wass . . ."

The look on Hustle's face was grim.

"What the hell happened? What he say?"

Hustle mumbled "hey" and kept walking. Mr. Freeman followed him with his eyes. Was it a girl? Police trouble?

"Hustle!"

He reversed course.

"What's happening? Lost your winning Lotto ticket?"

"Where's Mom?" asked Hustle, avoiding the question.

"She's out at one of her Girls' Night In dinners."

Ride took advantage of the moment to close his book slowly. "I'ma make me a fried bologna sandwich. Y'all want one?"

His father wasn't *that* distracted. "Sure, make us both one. Then finish your homework."

Mr. Freeman repeated his question, making room on the couch next to him. "What's going on, son? Come sit down. You in trouble again?"

Again? Hustle bristled. Why he have to come out his mouth like that? People acted like he was a career criminal.

"No, I'm not *in trouble*."

"Then trouble must be *in you*, because you're oozing it."

Hustle slumped on the couch. The rich, smoky aroma of meat cooking filled the apartment.

"I got shook down."

The words were said in a soft whisper, as if he didn't want to hear the truth of what had happened. "Remember the rap I wrote and paid all that money to make into a demo?"

Ride arrived, carrying a plate of sandwiches in one hand and a pitcher of grape Kool-Aid in the other.

Hustle described running into Pranksta, the balcony attack, the contract he'd signed. Ride grew agitated, interrupting the story to make threats against Motta and promises of vengeance to Hustle. When he was done, Hustle sighed. "I'm a sucka."

"No you ain't, that *sucka's* a sucka who need to get *popped*." Ride squeezed his trigger finger.

"*What?*" Mr. Freeman slammed down his sandwich.

"If I ever hear of you so much as *looking* too hard at a pistol, I will break each of your ten fingers, then start on your toes."

The boys exchanged guilty glances.

"Don't blame yourself, Eric. What can you do against a mob guy? You went for yours, that's the important thing. Believe me, if I could put two words together to a beat, I'd rap too. Don't get me wrong, I'm against all this gangster mess. Walk through the emergency room at Harlem Hospital any weekend, and it's full of shot-up, half-dead wannabe gangbangers."

"Least they other half still alive," said Ride.

"It's not funny, Lee. Look at your friend down the block—what's his name?—he was in your block patrol group. He'll be in that wheelchair for the rest of his life and he's still a teenager."

For once, Ride didn't have a joke. He was with Double Fo' at the Mitchel Houses block party, solid Crips turf, when some Bloods stormed it. Bullets flew like pellets from a child's BB gun. Except that *these* children had AKs, 357s, nines, and fofos. Medgar "Double Fo' " Hill, himself a fan of the *fofo*, or .44 Magnum, was hit several times. The bullet that struck his spine had barely missed Ride. Medgar was rarely seen after that, except occasionally when he was being raised and lowered on the wheelchair lift of a hospital van.

Gangs weren't new to New York and, indeed, have

been around for thousands of years. The word *thug* was first used in India in A.D. 1200 to describe buck-wilding hoodlums called Thugz. Just like the bangers who shot Double Fo', the Thugz had their own symbols, hand signs, rituals, and slang. Eight hundred years later, other buck-wilding hoodlums, inmates on Rikers Island, formed the United Blood Nation and replaced spears, bows, and arrows with semiautomatics. They chose red clothing, their rival gang the Crips chose blue, and a fashion tragedy was made.

Hustle said most dudes was only frontin' as gangstas anyway. Mr. Freeman disagreed. "Take somebody like Snoop Dogg, who's an idol for so many young kids. He's in these music videos with a blue kerchief in his back left pocket, calling himself a Crip and bragging about his AK-47. Shame on him. But you gotta give credit where credit's due, these young brothers—and sisters—are producing music, owning labels, and making money."

Ride smirked. "MC Hammer's broke, and that homeboy had *millions*. Forty-*fo'*, to be exact."

His father couldn't refute that. "True, but Hammer blew his on Arabian horses and sports teams, and hiring half the hood. Look at my generation. The record companies got rich while the singers fought for every dime. One of the Supremes died on welfare! Even then the business was dirty with payola, drugola, you name it. Where there's big money, there's always bigger crooks, and if this guy's mixed up with criminals like you say, maybe you got off easy."

"I ain't scared of that old punk," said Hustle, anger reviving his energy. "I'll step to anybody. Like a man."

"You know, you *think* you're Mr. Tough Guy, but you're just a kid. And the Tony Mottas of this world eat guys like you for dessert. You gotta let this thing go. Like a man. One with some common sense."

Hustle said he couldn't do that.

Over their bologna sandwich dinner, they discussed and rejected several options, including calling the police, threatening Pranksta, going to court, and sending someone after Motta. Then Ride hit on an idea.

"What about that white dude from the Tuff party? Ain't his father the boss of all them companies? Maybe *he* can bust some heads."

Hustle snapped his fingers. "That's right! He owns Tuff Roller, BullsEye, Pranksta, *everything*. And Motta's the one who said the corporate dudes is the big dawgs." He gave Ride a pound. "You can be *so* bugged, but when you're on . . . *whoa!*"

Mr. Freeman said that just might be the way to go.

"Ugh! What's the burnt smell?" asked Mrs. Freeman, sniffing the air as she came in. When she heard the story, it took a lot of persuading to stop her from calling the police on the spot. She said the bum should be locked up. A vote was taken, and it was settled that Hustle would try to get in touch with Mr. Adams.

That night Hustle lay on his mattress, exhausted but awake. He pockets a nice chain, he thought, then he gets jacked—by girls. Jeannette likes him, her grandmother hates him. One minute it's blowup time, then he's getting pushed off a balcony. Ups and downs. Too much roller coastering. Like shadows blending into night, his dark thoughts merged into a single black depression. No parents, passed around, lockdown, broke down, just plain *down*. He asked the air what he'd done, what he was being made to pay for. Ditching school? Stealing? Fighting? Wildin'? Sure he'd messed up, but who hadn't? The way he saw it, he was just surviving, struggling to be one of the fittest, one of the illest.

The way Darwin would have seen it, Hustle belonged to a very endangered species—young black guys with no schooling, no jobs, and lengthening rap sheets. But unlike the doomed mountain lion creeping inevitably towards extinction, Hustle had the power to change his destiny. But first, he had to believe it.

Finally asleep, he dreamed of a crowded outdoor stadium. The spectators went wild when he stepped into the throwing circle in a red do-rag, a black sleeveless nylon top, and green, form-fitting shorts. In his gloved hand he held a rope with a handle at one end and a large ball at the other. Under thunderclaps of applause, he swung the ball round and round his head, rotating his whole body, spinning at a blinding speed. He released the handle. The head of Tony Motta went flying through the air, his ponytail fluttering like the tail of a kite. The stadium roared. Hustle was the new hammer throw champion.

17

JEANNETTE WELCOMED THE RING OF HER WORK PHONE.
Anything that took her from the task of summarizing "A Wave from the Grave," a manuscript about the afterlife of royals, was a godsend.

"Jeannette Simpson."

" 'Sup?"

"Hustle?"

"I see you know my voice."

"It's more like I don't get too many people greeting me at work with 'sup.' So *wassup* with you?"

He wanted to hook up for lunch. Something had happened. Nah, nothing with the cops. They agreed to meet beneath the giant lingerie model.

Jeannette saw him waiting on the corner, his head up-turned.

"Yep, she's still there and you're still fiendin'."

They kissed their hellos.

"You rockin' Von *Duuuutch*?" He examined her jeans and lightweight, fitted jacket.

"It was a gift," she said. "I don't do brand names unless they're marked *waaay* down. Nanna says spending that much money on—"

"I'm sure Nanna say a lot about everything. But hey, she cool. She definitely gets you thinking."

She told him they'd talked a lot after he left and Nanna had come around—some—even admitting that she'd been biased against him from the beginning.

"So we all did some thinking," she said, "and that's always good. Now what's the big emergency and where're we eating?"

They stood at the counter of a fast-food restaurant. Hustle wanted the phone number of her friend Spence. She was curious to know why.

"You know the rap I wrote about you, the one you and Nanna hated—"

"I didn't *hate* it—"

"You *did*, don't lie. So anyway, I hook up the demo for Motta, but he's steady iggin' me. So I show up at his place to find out why he ain't got back to me. The dude's kinda scared . . . apologizing and making excuses."

He ate some cheeseburger.

"What's trippy is that right from the get-go I was pickin' up this vibe like he was gonna be trife."

"Trife?"

"Trouble. It was wrote all over him. Wassup with people? They make a deal then they wanna back out."

She was puzzled. "But when you first talked about him you seemed a hundred percent—"

He cut her off, embarrassed by his early enthusiasm. "Not really. I was on a positive tip right then, but I was always about laying back, checking him out. So it's about to go *down* 'cause I put my cash into the demo and I'm ready for my career to jump off. But he can't make it happen, so I say point-blank, 'f'git it.' Then I bounce. End of story. Except that I gotta get my demo back and he's crying and whining saying he can't find it."

He was pretty satisfied with his account.

"What a jerk. You should sue."

"Courtroom drama's for TV. You know me, I'm Emcee Plan B. The new deelio is that I'ma deal with the big wheelio, go to the CEO like I shoulda from the gitty-go."

"You're right, maybe Spence's father can do something. I'll get Spence's phone number from my boss. She's his aunt."

A table opened up. Jeannette had more she wanted to say about his visit. "You stirred up a lot of *issues*, let's say."

He started to speak, but she interrupted. "Not so much about rap. I mean, I know she's right about the negative messages and all that, but I'm not hard-core like her. I get hooked by the dance beat and next thing I'm singing along. Take Pranksta's song . . ."

The name brought a frown to his face.

"The words are stupid, but the music's—"

"Pranksta's wack."

"He *so* is. And his sister is the *nerdiest* black kid there ever was, probably since Condoleezza Rice was a teenager."

A woman walking past overheard the comment and burst out laughing.

"The main issue that came up was how Nanna has too close a hold on me because of my folks. My mom never comes around, and my father . . . who knows? So Nanna's overprotective. She never likes any boy I have over."

"What? You got *other* dudes?" He slammed his fist in his palm.

"Right. Keep playing. The point is that she wants you to know you're welcome in her home. And that . . . let me see if I remember this right . . . she's not thrilled about the destination but admires your drive. And so do I."

"I'm down with that."

"But . . . now don't take this the wrong way . . ."

"I ain't." He braced himself.

"I'm *not*," said Jeannette.

"You ain't what?"

"You *aren't* what."

"Aren't what, *what*? What's wrong with you? You eat something funny?"

"It's 'aren't,' not 'ain't.' Nanna doesn't like your English."

"You said she like me."

"She *does*. But she *is* a teacher. And you're always saying 'ain't,' 'aight,' 'I'ma.' She says you talk *thuglish*—thug English. If you would just *try* to speak . . . different . . . it would give her one less thing to bug about."

Hustle waved her off. "I get it. I ain't good enough for her precious private school baby 'cause I don't talk white? I talk how I talk 'cause I'm *blacklikedat*."

"Oh, like I'm not? Look, Money, I kicks it with my homegirls straight up project, you know what I'm sayin'? But when I *want* to, I *can* talk regular standard English. 'Cause I'm bilingual *likedat*. West *Siiiide*." Her hoodie pose, arms folded on her chest and her fingers forming a *W*, gave them both a good laugh.

Mrs. Simpson was a trip, but if his saying "aren't" meant she'd cut them some slack, hey, it was just a word. He tapped out a beat on the table. "I'ma kick a freestyle for you, listen up—

111

"Your granny called Nanny wanna bust me with no
*   warrant*
'cause I be sayin' 'ain't' when she always sayin' 'aren't'
but she don't really fool me 'cause she steady trynna
*   school me*
to talk all like a scooby from that movie Scooby-
Dooby."

"Exactly, Hustle! So just try it, *pleeeze*."

It was time to return to the tales of beheaded monarchs. She handed him a book. "From Nanna. I've had it here for a while and was gonna give you a call about getting together for lunch, but you beat me to it."

18

CERTAINLY HE REMEMBERED HIM, WHISPERED SPENCE.
Open Mic at the Crib, yes, yes . . . the Tuff Roller party, of course.

The family chef stood at the maple dining table, patiently waiting for the end of the call. He held a platter of Maine lobster and rock shrimp with mixed baby greens. They had begun with an appetizer of glazed oysters topped with caviar.

"Not at the table, dear," said Dorothy "Dot" Stowbridge Adams, a slim socialite with dark hair, darker eyes, and a tendency to swing into some very dark moods.

"Then that *puto* gonna step to me and try to throw my black butt off the balcony! You *feel* me?"

"Uh, sure, I do feel it, I definitely do," said Spence,

grimacing in a way that was meant to convey he was *trying* to get off the phone.

"Dear," said Mrs. Adams, an edge in her voice, "Pierre's holding a heavy tray and your father and I would like to continue our meal."

"So, Suspence, money respect money, right? What I'm trying to say is, Can you hook me up with your pops? I need him to back me up with Motta. If he help me out now, when I *do* blow, I'ma remember y'all. Anybody'll tell you, my word is *bond*."

"End the call, Spencer," ordered his father. "You're upsetting your mother. *Now*."

"Sure . . . okay . . . say, a week from Friday? Excellent, gotta go." Spence clicked off his phone and served himself. Pierre disappeared into the kitchen.

"I thought I told you to instruct your friends not to call during the dinner hour."

"You did, Dad. Sorry. That wasn't a friend, it was . . . uh . . . kind of school-related."

"Oh, that's wonderful," enthused Mrs. Adams. "Is Harvard recruiting you for the Krokodiloes? As well they should, you have such a rich tenor."

Spence busied himself with the succulent lobster.

Mr. Adams dabbed his mouth with his cloth napkin before speaking. "When I was there, I managed to finagle admission to the Hasty Pudding Club, but the Kroks didn't make the same mistake. The first note out of my mouth shrieked 'tone-deaf.' Instant rejection."

Spencer Adams *père*, still fit and handsome in his early sixties, had enjoyed a privileged upbringing in Boston. He'd attended Phillips Academy and Harvard, elite private schools with annual tuitions ten times an average Harlem family's yearly income. After graduation, he had to find a job. As his unwavering good fortune would have it, one awaited him at the corporation founded by his grandfather.

All that remained was for him to fill in the details of his preordained life. This he did with a trophy wife and three Harvard sons housed in an Upper East Side town house. He added a Mercedes-Benz sedan, a Sunseeker yacht, a Bombardier Learjet, and, his most prized possession, a Concord watch with a brown alligator strap and an eighteen-karat yellow-gold and diamond case.

A respectable amount of philanthropy crowned it all with scholarships, foundations, and art endowments bearing the Adams name. A charitable opportunity like none he'd ever imagined was about to present itself.

Mrs. Adams complimented the chef's cherries jubilee dessert, her favorite throughout the year. "But it *will* add another half hour to tomorrow's workout. It's infernal how vigilant a woman my age has to be just to fit into a simple Chanel suit."

Dot Adams was the sort of woman who kept her age a mystery by endless pampering, and the rare but absolutely necessary surgical tweak from time to time. The Wellesley alumna fought off the ravages of childbirth and the creep of age like a competitive athlete. Pilates, aerobics, and yoga furiously practiced with a personal trainer in the fitness center of the family residence consumed hours of her day. When not exercising, she appeared at parties, took vacations, and attended meetings of museum boards.

Spencer Sr. knew when a compliment was in order. "Dot, you're lovely at any age."

Spencer Jr. also knew. "Mom, you have nothing to worry about, you're a total hottie." He scooped some cherry sorbet onto his spoon.

"Spence, you know how I feel about such language. Fletcher still teaches its students English, I assume. Go on, dazzle me with your grasp of it."

"You're superb, Mother, exquisite."

"Much better," she said, fluttering her eyes playfully. Then she remembered the irritating phone call.

"You never answered my question, dear. Was that a Krok on the phone?"

Spence filled his mouth with more sorbet.

She looked at him pointedly. "Who *was* that?"

"A guy, that's all."

"From Fletcher? Harvard? How's it school related?"

Spence's parents raised their eyebrows disapprovingly. On their minds was another phone call, the one they'd received after Thanksgiving from Fletcher's headmaster regarding their son's pot dealing. After all, said Mr. Clement, also a family friend, the boy was beginning Harvard in the fall, and they might not be as lenient as Fletcher with respect to a young man sowing his wild oats. As punishment, Spence was grounded in New York for the summer and forbidden to accompany his brothers on their Nepal trek. The same question troubled them both: Was he at it again? Was that what the mystery phone call was about? They certainly thought so.

His mother could barely contain her fury. "What *is* it with you, Spencer? Do you realize you're jeopardizing your future, your whole *life*?" Her breath was coming in short gasps.

His father regarded him sternly. "Look at your poor mother, Spencer. Don't force my hand on this one. I thought grounding you would suffice to teach you a lesson, but if I must—"

"That's it." A slight tremble was in her voice. "I'm making an appointment with Dr. Baum. She's the best shrink there is for *disturbed* "—she lingered over the word—"adolescents."

Spence grimaced. Sure he'd sold a little pot around campus, but it was only pot, and only to friends, and only for fun. Besides, he'd given them his word.

"Mom, Dad, it's not *that*. I said I'd stop and I did. That was a singer on the phone, a rapper actually, whom I met—"

His mother swallowed. "A . . . *rapper?*"

"—at a Tuff Roller event. He's my age. We didn't talk much, but he seemed okay, in his own way."

"What does a rapper want with you?" asked his father, less disturbed by the R word than his wife. He didn't think much of the music, but the after-tax profits of Tuff Roller Records, Inc., had tripled in the past two years.

"Nothing. He wants *you*."

"Your *father?*" Mrs. Adams sensed a threat hovering over her family.

"It's nothing bad. Tony Motta scammed him for one of his songs, and he wants Dad to intervene."

"I don't micromanage AGE subsidiaries. What's the kid's name, anyway? Is he successful?"

"I don't know his real name. He goes by Hustle."

His mother wiped her mouth. "*Hustle?* Oh, *Spence*. Does he wear that hideous face jewelry?"

Spence ignored the question.

"From what I understand, he's just starting out. He has a lot of heart. I guess he's trying to find a way out of Harlem."

"*Harlem?*" She looked pleadingly towards Heaven and was momentarily distracted and soothed by the sight of her polished brass and crystal two-tier chandelier.

Spence loved his mother, but at times she drove him up a wall. And this was one of those times.

"Yes, Mom, he's a black dude from Harlem named Hustle who raps and wears his baseball cap backward."

She took a large sip of Calvados. "Don't use that tone with me, Spencer Adams."

"Spencer," said Mr. Adams.

This rebellious side of Spence was very distasteful to her. She promised herself to call Dr. Baum, first thing. She ventured another question. "You don't like that kind of . . . *music* . . . do you?"

"No way," claimed Spence, "you know I'm a Joss Stone kinda guy."

"Well, thank God for *that*."

Mr. Adams cracked all his knuckles at once. "Maybe it *would* be interesting to see how the other half lives."

"The other *half*, Dad? My multiculturalism prof said the *majority* of the world's population is poor."

Mr. Adams shook his head. "Is *that* what I'm paying thirty grand a year for you to learn?"

Pierre entered and asked if there would be anything else. He could clear the table, said Mrs. Adams, they were done.

"Sure," said Mr. Adams, "I'll meet the kid."

"Spencer!"

"He's a friend of our son's, darling, and he needs help." He looked at Spence. "Does he golf?"

"Very funny, Dad. I *said* he's up in Harlem."

"So's Bill Clinton. And I've golfed with *him*."

A bead of sweat slipped down the back of Mrs. Adams's neck. She addressed her husband in a chilly, calm voice. "And why don't we have him join us at the Hampton Horse Show? He could perform one of his rap tunes in the VIP Patrons' Tent."

She sprang to her feet, knocking to the floor her hand-carved, upholstered chair. She slammed the dining room door behind her, rattling a china set in the cabinet.

19

HUSTLE DODGED BUSES AND CARS SPEEDING ALONG CENTRE Street and entered a nondescript office building. He passed through a weapons detector and pushed into a packed elevator. At 2, the door opened onto a large wall sign: N.Y.S. Division of Probation and Correctional Alternatives. The office could've been holding auditions for *American Rap Idol.* The acre of do-rags alone, if stitched together, could easily have made an opulent silk wedding gown. And there were enough gold and silver crosses to dress an entire sanctified congregation. Young men were playing cards, bouncing to music, text-messaging on cells, and otherwise chilling out as they waited lightheartedly for another month of conditional freedom. The rows of metal chairs were full, so after signing in with the receptionist, Hustle leaned next to a wall poster of Martin Luther King, Jr.'s "I Have a Dream" speech. Underneath was posted a Justice Department statistic: "1 out of 3 African-American men aged 20 to 29 is in prison, on probation or on parole." Someone had written "cops" across "African-American men" and "should be" over "is."

"Samson." The receptionist yawned. "Samson, Eric."

Hustle's probation officer, Angelina Contreras, was making notes on her last case when he walked in.

"You made it. I hoped you wouldn't force me to pay you a personal visit. You *know* how much I hate field trips."

And for good reason. Probation officers who went out in the field to locate wayward probationers sometimes had to fight off pit bulls, chase down sprinters, and duck bullets. She'd laid down the law from the outset. Even one no-show was an automatic violation that could send him to jail. Two years earlier, she had been a business lawyer who chose to cut her salary by four-fifths with the vague goal of "helping people." A South Bronx native and Park Slope resident, she was an inner-city success story and hoped to share her blessings with others. Her fantasy of playing social worker to contrite criminals evaporated the moment she was handed a nine-millimeter Glock pistol and told to begin handgun training classes.

"Ain't missed a face-to-face in five months, have I? I

got caught up in a couple of things. But the month ain't over."

"What kinds of things? You're keeping your nose clean, right?" She pushed curly, dark hair from her eyes as if better to read his face.

"Right." Hustle kept his P.O. at arm's length. Black, white, Hispanic, it didn't matter. He drew no distinction between probation officers and cops. Few probationers did. If it wore a badge, carried a gun, and could get you locked up, it was Five-O.

"Still reside with the Freeman family?"

"Yes."

"And that's still okay?"

"Yes."

"No shoplifting?"

"Nope."

"No vandalism?"

"Nope."

"No drugs?"

"Nope. You *know* I don't do drugs."

"Sorry. My bad. But *you* know I have to ask. My job's to make sure you stay out of trouble while under the court's supervision."

"The answer's still no."

"Good. Looking for work?"

"Yes. Rap. I'm writing rhymes."

She sighed. *All* her probationers were writing rhymes. All the teenagers in her *family* were writing rhymes.

"Uh-huh. You might want to think about a Plan B. The rap rainbow leads to very few pots of gold. I hear the post office is hiring."

"Uh-huh. I'll check it out."

"Right," she said skeptically. "You got anything else for me?"

"Nope."

"Then we'll see you next month."

"Yes."

Outside, the twin towers that once reflected the pinks and reds of evening were long gone. But the neighborhood at the tip of Manhattan was back. Government workers in the Federal Building. Local powerbrokers at City Hall. Cops streaming in and out of their New York headquarters at One Police Plaza. His favorite music store, the fancy hotels he dreamed about, the pizza joints he liked . . . the city had overcome and resurrected. And the subliminal suggestion of that renewal wasn't lost on Hustle. He too had a dream. And all the *post office* had for him was stamps. For himself, he had his writing, the Freemans, maybe Jeannette. His steps fell into the busy rhythm of the rush-hour crowd as he joined the march towards the maze of the Fulton Street subway stop.

20

WHEN HUSTLE WALKED IN, MRS. FREEMAN WAS HAVING her hair done by a neighborhood girl fresh from Atlanta.

"Moms, wassup?" said Hustle. "Hey, *shooorty*." He watched the girl's cheeks turn red. "When them little country fingers gonna hook me up with some cornrows?"

"When you grow some hair," she drawled with a giggle, her voice high and babyish.

"All right now, Eric," warned Mrs. Freeman without having to say more. "You met with the lady?"

"I saw her. She was sweatin' me with the same wack questions every visit, *Still reside with the Freemans? Looking for work?* Like I'd tell her anything anyway."

"She's only doing her job. Did you tell her what happened with that bum? Maybe she can help you out."

"I ain't tell her nothing. She'd probably try to bust me for consorting with a known jerk or some such violation." The apartment was quiet. "Where Ride?"

The woman checked out her braids in the mirror. "Why these so loose, Tiffany? You have to redo them, honey." Hustle's question dawned on her. "Ride and his father are out with the new father-son group from the church. I saved you a pork chop, and there's some fried okra in there too."

Hustle stood in silence for a moment. What father-son group? He shook off the feeling. "I ain't hungry."

"Suit yourself," she said, catching his reflection in the mirror. She'd *told* Man to wait for that boy.

The room had a stuffy, closed-in feeling. He turned on a fan, unwrapped a candy bar, stretched out gingerly on his mattress so as not to cause a dust storm, and began writing:

> *uptown it goes down, fellas hittin' red ground*
> *for nothin'*
> *Glock-rockin' awe-shockin' soldiers on the wrong*
> *   battleground*
> *ain't nothin'*
> *the Five-O's, the P.O.'s, got us all on lockdown*
> *we nothin'*

He reread the lyrics, smiled, then noticed the present from Nanna. The book, *Notable African-American Poets*, was where he'd tossed it—on a pile of clothes. Inside, a handwritten inscription: "For Hustle—Poets are rappers without beats, rappers are rarely poets. May you find your muse somewhere in these lines. Keep hustling. Create peace, Nanna Simpson." He looked up *muse* in the dictionary he kept nearby: ". . . any of the nine sister Greek goddesses presiding over song and poetry and the arts and sciences; a source of inspiration . . ."

Songs he had, but poems . . . he wasn't sure. He began reading. It took a rumble in his stomach to make him realize how long he'd been at it. That, and the sudden ruckus that announced Ride's return.

"Ma said you was in here. Hey, I *told* Man to wait and take you with us, but he was stressin' about being late. What you doin'?"

"I ain't mad atcha, homey. I'm chillin' with this book. What y'all do?"

Ride cut him a look that said everything. "Boy, it was a wack attack. Mondy had us sitting in a circle like Girl Scouts, then we was s'pose to talk about goals and fears. Lame. Nothin' but dudes and they daddies. I was like, where the movie at? They finally showed it right there in the church! And here I am thinking we was going to Magic Johnson's movie house. They didn't have no popcorn, nachos, pizza, hot dogs . . . not even a Jaw-breaker. I wasn't even trynna feel no Antwone Fisher story about this black orphan Navy dude talking in Chinese."

Ride dropped onto the bed, stirring dust.

"What I tell you about that, man!"

"What I tell *you*? *Vacuum* this stank-nasty dustpan. Why you readin'? *You* ain't the one gettin' left back."

"It's aight. Listen to this rhyme about some pool sharks."

Tapping out a beat, he recited from memory,

We real cool. We
Left school. We

Lurk late. We
Strike straight. We

Sing sin. We
Thin gin. We

Jazz June. We
Die soon.

He stopped. "Ain't that the illest?"

"Like I always be sayin', you kick nothin' *but* dope rhymes."

Hustle showed him the book. "It ain't mine, son, it's in here. This old black lady name Gwendolyn Brooks wrote it a long time ago."

"You *lyin'*. Now old black ladies being emcees?"

"Here's a funny one, about this wild girl name Kissie Lee.

"Well Kissie Lee took her advice
And after that she didn't speak twice
'Cause when she learned to stab and run
She got herself a little gun.
And from that time that gal was mean,
Meanest mama you ever seen.
She could hold her likker and hold her man
And she went thoo life jus' raisin' san'."

"Don't tell me a little old lady rapper wrote that too."

"Margaret Walker in the house," said Hustle. "I woulda loved to hear *them* two battle."

"Ain't no dudes in that book?"

"Claude McKay, Langston Hughes . . . a young dude named Saul Williams, who spits his poems like a rapper. He got a line about a girl with eyes like two turntables. Boy gettin' *paid* too, and ain't no criminals tryin' to throw *him* off no balcony."

Ride wanted to know who gave Hustle the book.

"Jeannette's grandmother. She wanna educate me, make me talk English right."

"Don't be comin' around me talkin' white."

Hustle's attempt at an English accent sounded like Austin Powers drunk. "I don't intend no such thing, Manley, my good man. As your ignorant self do know, coffee don't turn you black and talking right can't make you white."

"You need help—a shot of Jack or a long talk with Minister Mondy. But you definitely need help."

"Jeannette wants me to speak better too."

"So you sayin' if you talk pretty, she gon' give up the nasty?"

"Why you gotta . . . ?" He shoulder-tackled Ride, and they crashed onto the mattress. A cloud of skin flakes and dust mites billowed around them. Coughing and hungry, they raced to the kitchen. Hustle's laughter ended abruptly when he saw Mr. Freeman finishing the last pork chop. All that remained of dinner were a few lukewarm stalks of mushy okra.

21

SPENCER ADAMS'S "WEEK FROM FRIDAY" FELT MORE LIKE a year. Hustle hit St. Nicholas Park in the afternoons for pickup basketball, played cards at tables set up on the street, cruised the neighborhood. He read, he wrote, sometimes he'd call Jeannette just to say hello. But he couldn't invite her anywhere, being almost broke. Boosting was over—the threat of jail was all too intimidating. He *had* to find a way to get paid. And he wanted the money for "Back-Seat Shorty." The wait had become almost unbearable when Friday arrived.

Mrs. Freeman was preparing that evening's dinner. She always started early when they were having fish because it took so long to clean. Mr. Freeman himself had caught the striped bass off the 125th Street Terminus overlooking the Hudson River. It was a family favorite, which is why she was surprised by Hustle's announcement that he wouldn't be eating with them.

"I already got a dinner rendez-vous."

"Rendez-vous?" asked Mrs. Freeman. "Well, aren't *you* just all high and mighty with your French talk."

"He just *high*, if you ask me," said Ride.

"Nobody *asked* you, Manley," snapped Mr. Freeman, "and what do you know about getting high? Don't *let* me find out . . ."

"I ain't messin' with nothin'. Why you always gotta sweat me?"

His father gave him a look, then his mother directed her own menacing look his way.

"Remember? I meet the Adams family today!"

"Tell Gomez and Morticia I said hi," joked Ride. "Give my boy Pugsley a shout too."

"Yes, I *do* remember, Eric. It came so fast. Good luck. I hope they hang that bum high."

"Keep your head on straight now, like a man," said Mr. Freeman.

The doorbell chimed with soft welcome. Mrs. Adams rushed to the fitness center, vowing to remain there until the visitor had departed. A man with carefully groomed gray hair, a distinguished bearing, and a fine suit answered the door. Hustle grabbed his hand.

"Wassup . . . I mean, hello. I'm glad to meet you, Mr. Adams, and I just want to thank you for . . ."

A slight twitch in the corner of his mouth was the only reaction the butler allowed himself to show. "Please come this way, sir. Mr. Adams and Spencer are expecting you."

"Oh shi—" Hustle caught himself.

Making their way to the grand salon, they moved beneath the vaulted ceiling of the vestibule, across oak floors with mahogany paneling, past a Louis XV chest with hand-painted floral designs.

"The guest has arrived," announced Cyril with somewhat exaggerated flourish.

Traveling from Harlem, that guest had been forced to take a crosstown bus to Lexington Avenue, hop a southbound subway train, then double back westward on foot to reach the Adamses' nine-million-dollar home, a nineteenth-century town house with arched windows and a tall chimney.

Why he had to take such a circuitous route in a borough served from its Inwood Hill head to its Battery Park toe by an extensive grid of subway track had everything to do with the social activism of Mrs. Adams and her neighbors. Years earlier they had joined together, protested to politicians, and lobbied through lawyers in a fevered bid to block a proposed westward extension of the East

Side–Lexington Avenue subway line. Speaking at a cocktail dinner organized for the occasion by the socialite Chloë Cavendish of Cavendish Resorts, Dot Adams evoked the specter of musty, rumbling trains bringing unseemly individuals to the very doorsteps of the Upper East Side. Why in heaven's name did they need a subway when every one of them owned at least two luxury cars?

Spence greeted Hustle with a handshake.

"Hi. So we meet again." He lowered his voice. "I'm Spence here, not Suspence, okay?"

Seeing Hustle bop into the salon and imagining his mother upstairs freaking out on her elliptical machine made him giggle. Mr. Adams was also on his feet and shook Hustle's hand. Indicating a russet leather chair, he invited him to *"please . . . sit."*

"Mr. Adams, meeting you means a lot to me, man, and I just wanna thank you for helping me out in this . . . uh . . . situation."

There was a disarming pathos about the young man, thought Mr. Adams.

"My son has spoken highly of you . . . er . . . Hustle. Is that your real name?"

"Nah . . . no. It's Eric. Eric Samson. People started calling me that because I always had a hustle going, you know, trying to get paid."

He relaxed into the deep, soft chair.

"I'm with you a hundred percent on that one, Eric.

You don't mind if I call you by your given name, do you? I'm a little old-fashioned when it comes to those things."

"Hey, old school cool too."

Spencer made a coughing sound to disguise his laughter.

"Generating and maintaining a steady revenue stream is such a challenge these days, isn't it? What *is* your line of business, in fact?" Mr. Adams shot a warning glare at his son.

"Retail," responded Hustle without a flinch. "I get clothes wholesale and sell 'em to private clients. And music."

Mr. Adams smoothed his hair. "I see."

"Speaking of music, that's a *monster*," said Hustle, noticing the Schimmel grand piano at the far end of the salon. "Who play? You, Susp— uh . . . Spence?"

"My mom."

"Now, Spence," said his proud father, "no false humility. Eric, our son has been studying with Gustave— with one of the top instructors for more than a decade. His mother's also a classically trained pianist. Her interpretations of Schubert and Debussy are truly exquisite."

"Cool. So where she at? I wanna meet her too."

"Sleeping," blurted Spence.

"Reading," said Mr. Adams at the same time.

"I *feel* that. Sometimes I fall asleep reading too."

22

MR. ADAMS PRESSED A REMOTE, AND A DIFFERENT SER-vant appeared.

"Pierre. Refreshments. Thank you."

Hustle looked from father to son. "Y'all really look a lot alike. Kinda like Austin Powers and Mini-Me."

Spence seemed to wince.

"Don't get me wrong, I mean that in a good way!"

Spence asked how Hustle knew his school friend Nathaniel Whitely.

"Me and Schoolie? We been tight from day one. Raised up on the same block."

"Interesting," observed Mr. Adams, "how you pursued such different paths."

"School wasn't never my thing. I was more . . . business-oriented."

"I see."

Pierre rolled in a pastry trolley.

"Help yourselves, Eric, Spence. I'm watching my weight."

Hustle took a chocolate éclair. Mr. Adams asked to hear the story of Hustle's rap song. By the time Hustle had finished the tale, he'd also finished a second éclair, an almond croissant, and a mound of pistachio nuts.

"I see," said Mr. Adams again.

He suggested Spence entertain the guest while he made some calls.

Spencer Adams, Jr.'s recreation room was twice the size of the Freeman apartment. A sixty-inch plasma flat-screen TV monitor connected to a high-definition satellite dish offered four hundred channels. His sixty-disc CD-MP3 player and a DVD jukebox did more than justice to his enormous music collection, which included a secret stash of rap. The sound from the four-foot speakers was crisper than any Hustle had heard. In a corner were lacrosse sticks and next to them a case of handcrafted pool cues. But Hustle wasn't interested in shooting pool. His eyes were on the gaming consoles.

"This not nobody's *room*," he said, trying to get in the

habit of not saying "ain't." "This a whole *store*. Game-Cube, Xbox, PlayStation2 . . . wow. What games you got?"

"You name it. I have a hundred fifty at this house, and probably another fifty or sixty in our East Hampton place. Here, take this." Spence handed him a PlayStation controller. Sitting on futons, they began playing Need for Speed Underground, losing themselves in the vivid graphics as they tore through urban streets in customized cars.

In his upstairs study, Mr. Adams was conversing heatedly on a cell phone.

"I'm no lawyer, but I *do* know about *respondeat superior*. In these matters, and you'll pardon the reference, sewage always floats upstream. Threatening to throw people from balconies is *not* an AGE business practice! Motta was so far outside the scope of professional behavior he might as well have been on the moon!"

Maxwell English, general counsel for Adams Global Electronics, was speaking from his vacation home in the Caribbean, where he'd hoped to have a restful ten days. He couldn't help but be skeptical about the outlandish story. Was Spencer absolutely sure the incident had happened?

"Of *course* it did! I phoned around, and apparently this is the way the guy operates. Samson? He's just a naïve

Harlem kid, you know the type, pants halfway falling off, aspiring rapper, the whole nine yards."

English was worried about a possible criminal complaint against Motta and the inevitable expensive civil lawsuit naming Tuff Roller, BullsEye, and AGE.

"We can count our lucky stars on this one, Max. So far, not a syllable about litigation, damages, nothing. All he wants is his song back, and I can take care of that end of it. But Motta has to go, and I don't give a damn about his employment contract. You're the lawyer, find a way to get him out. Pay him off if you have to. I want him gone, and I mean *yesterday*."

The study door swung open as he hung up. Dot was sweaty in pink low-rise Lycra pants and a matching sport bra.

"What's going on?" she asked. "I heard you raise your voice. Is everything all right? Where's Spence? Is that *man* still here?" She sounded panicky.

Her husband explained the company's predicament. "We could have some exposure here, so we have to play it real smart. As distasteful as it is to you, I'm going to need your support on this. He's an okay kid. A little cash and a pat on the back, and it all goes away. Right now, they're having a great time in the rec room. Look."

He stepped on the foot control, and a wall panel slid back, revealing two rows of monitors showing images from the street outside, the roof, and every room in the house. And there they were, Hustle and Spence in black and white, excitedly playing a video game.

"My!" she said.

"Funny, isn't it? You'd think they were best buddies."

"But he looks so . . . *dangerous*." She made a shivering sound.

"He's harmless, Dot. And he's staying for dinner. The kid's potentially holding a golden ax over my head. I can't risk some community activist lawyer getting wind of what happened and coming after us. You with me, Skipper?"

"Always, Captain."

Dot went upstairs to change.

23

"**IT'S ALWAYS A PLEASURE,**" **SAID DOROTHY STOWBRIDGE** Adams with all the courtesy she could muster, "to meet Spence's friends."

She'd chosen something casual, a Jones New York pipe red silk shirtdress, there being no reason to really dress.

"I was *hopin'* to meet the lady of the house."

"Um-hmm," she responded, her eyes fixed on her husband's cuff links. "Well! Let's eat, shall we? I hope your friend likes chops, Spence."

"I *love* me some pork chops, and Miss Freeman cooks 'em with apples. They are *good*."

"We're having lamb chops," she said, "if that's okay."

"Hungry as I am, I'd eat a *dog* chop."

She shuddered.

· · ·

The usual dining protocol was that guests be served first, then family. This dinner, however, was far from the usual. On the serving trolley simmered a platter of aged roasted lamb chops, white beans, and confit of leeks. Pierre pushed the trolley next to Hustle's chair and stopped.

"Nah, I can wait. Dish *her* up. As they say, ladies first."

Mrs. Adams's face briefly took on the color of her dress. Spence lowered his eyes. Mr. Adams signaled to Pierre to go ahead and serve Dot.

"Eric's right. As they say, beauty before the beasts."

"That's a good one, *heh heh*. I like that . . . beauty before the beasts, *heh heh*."

Unable to restrain himself, Spence began laughing.

Silverware clinked lightly as they dined. The boys compared video games and consoles. To her growing annoyance, Hustle complimented Mrs. Adams more than once on her cooking. Mr. Adams continued to affirm pleasantly whatever Hustle said. The topic of the moment was Hustle's distrust of the banking system.

"Now *that's* an interesting point, Eric. Don't you agree, Dot?"

She either didn't agree or hadn't heard, as she made no answer.

"I kid y'all not, I keeps my stash, when I *have* one, in a knit hat rolled up and stuck behind a crate. Me and banks, I just ain't . . . not . . . feeling it. Even when I was little, my cash stayed rolled in my pocket with a rubber band around it. Suppose the bank get robbed, *then* where your money at? I know you get it back, but how long *that* take?"

"If the Feds keep raising short-term interest rates, I may cash out of stocks and carry *my* dough rolled up in my pocket too, *hahaha*."

Spence groaned. "Dad, nobody says 'dough.' "

Mrs. Adams silently helped herself to another serving of leeks.

Mr. Adams shifted the conversation. "You know, Eric, as I think I mentioned, both Spence and my wife are gifted musicians. *You're* an artist as well. As for me, being about as musically gifted as a doorknob, I'm *fascinated* by the creative process. So tell me, how do you write a rap song? The story line, the tempo, where does it all come from?"

The dinner was beginning to challenge Mrs. Adams's social graces. "Dear, let our guest eat in peace. *Please*."

"Hey, I can eat and talk, no problem. Always glad to drop some knowledge about rap. I write about my reality, what I'm thinking about, you know. Then I kick the flow with some R & B on the hook, maybe a little oldie-goldie sampling, some phat beats, and *bam!* I'm ready to spit."

Mrs. Adams grunted softly, as though she'd felt a sudden sharp pain. Pierre entered and announced the dessert choices. Working on her second cucumber cosmo martini, Mrs. Adams declined.

Hustle didn't quite catch the menu. "Can you run that by me again?"

The chef repeated, "Black chocolate mousse with lemon and caramelized tangerine, warm apple pie with two creams, Black Forest gâteau with sugared bitter cherries and a white chocolate sauce."

"I think you'd like the chocolate cake," offered Spence, pointing to the Black Forest gâteau. "That's what I'll have, Pierre."

"Make that three," chimed in Mr. Adams, who rarely ate dessert but was intent on being in perfect harmony with their guest.

After dinner, Mrs. Adams complained of feeling "drained" and left the dining room with a rapid "nice meeting you." Mr. Adams asked his son if he'd mind leaving him and Eric alone to "talk privately." Spence shook Hustle's hand again and retreated to his room.

Then Spencer Adams, Sr., struck. He recited the opening lines of the scenario drawn up by the lawyer. "Eric, you're a businessman yourself, so I know I don't have to tell you that fair play is not always how our world operates."

"*That's* word."

"But it should. There are men like you and me, and

then there are guys like Tony Motta. Two different breeds. And what he did was more than unfair, it was plain wrong."

"I know, man."

"So I pulled a few strings."

Hustle made a fist. "Yes!"

"The contract you signed is a pile of ashes, and 'Back-Seat Sporty' is once again yours."

Hustle was so excited he didn't notice the mistake. "Now *that's* juice!"

Act One had gone exactly as Maxwell had predicted. Act Two might be trickier. Mr. Adams waited a moment to let the happy news sink in. "And that's not all"—he lowered his voice—"and this is totally against legal advice, since Mr. Motta is *solely* to blame for his actions."

He paused. So far so good.

"I want to personally compensate you for the unprofessional behavior of someone indirectly in my employ."

He poured himself some water and turned into the home stretch.

"I listened to your song over the phone, and it's pretty catchy. There is *no* way it's not worth double, no . . . *triple* what you asked for. No *way*."

He took a long sip from the glass, watching Hustle's expression. It was a done deal.

"Mr. Adams, that's . . . I-I don't know what to say, it's like . . ."

"Based on the song's actual value . . . Just take this check, son."

Hustle read it. Once. Again. His cool was crumbling under the heat of emotion. "Pay to the order of Eric Samson—three thousand dollars and no cents."

He flashbacked to the doorman, Pranksta, the cigar, the railing. Images swirled to mind like debris trapped in a tornado. Mr. Adams signed two typed pages he'd pulled from a folder.

"You know what I just did, my friend? I put this unpleasant incident behind us. Would you do me the honor . . ." He handed Hustle his pen. "The document simply summarizes what I just said, so we both have a record of it."

"You *more* than a friend," said Hustle, signing immediately, "you my *homey*."

Mr. Adams stuck out his hand. "Gimme five, homey."

Hustle left the Adams residence in complete joy, the Release from Liability and Settlement Agreement in hand.

Night had emptied the museums, shops, and restaurants of the Upper East Side. Mr. Adams, in silk striped pajamas and matching robe, was in his study having a nightcap when his son came in.

"You took advantage of him, didn't you?"

"Don't be silly, Spence. You didn't see his face when he left. He got three grand, a fortune to a guy like that."

"Sure, but *fifty* bucks is probably a lot to him. You know that if he'd sued—"

His father interrupted impatiently. "Oh, that's choice, Spence. So you'd prefer that some shyster lawyer play Lotto with the company founded by your great-grandfather, built by your grandfather, and run by your father."

"Of course not, Dad. But the case would've settled for fifty, seventy-five thou, right? His whole *life* would change, but for you it would be *nothing*, a deductible business expense."

Mr. Adams yawned. "The hour is late. I hope Harvard manages to teach you some basic Darwinian lessons. Like the fact that the lifestyle you were born into and currently enjoy is the result of our family's hard work and sacrifice. We were the fittest, and we reached the top. One day it'll be up to you and your brothers to remain there. Let others save the world, Spence, we're here to run it."

He tousled his son's blond hair. "Go get some sleep, we have a long drive to East Hampton in the morning. Good night, son."

"Good night, Dad."

24

HUSTLE TALKED ENDLESSLY ABOUT THE DINNER BUT DIDN'T mention the payment once, planning to surprise the Freemans with some money. So he set out to cash the check.

The man behind the one-way bulletproof glass window warned that there would be a 10 percent charge on all cashed checks, then reexamined the check Hustle had slid through the slot.

"I can't cash this anyway. This a personal check. How I know it's not stole? If you have a government check—social security, welfare, a tax refund, okay. But this"—he flipped it over and back again—"sorry, brother, no can do. Maybe try a bank . . ." He slid it back.

"Bank? If I had a bank account, I wouldn't be up in this rip-off joint. You know no bank's gonna cash a check from somebody walking in off the street. Why you gotta play me? I grew up right around the corner, everybody know my word is bond. The check's good."

He was steaming, but his pleas met deaf ears and indifferent eyes.

"I say no, brother. How I know this check got any money behind it?"

"You know what, *brother*? The dude who wrote this is a friend of mine who could buy your whole shady-ass business *and* your shady-ass wife."

He knocked a stack of EZ Check Cashing flyers to the floor on his way out.

Mrs. Freeman's eyes watered up when he told her about his wish to surprise her with a "donation." Sure, she said, she could deposit it and give him the money when the check cleared. But shouldn't he keep all that cash in a safe place? It took every skillful argument about house fires and break-ins she could come up with before he would agree to open a savings account. They went to her bank together and did the paperwork. Hustle liked the sight of "Eric Samson" embossed on his cash card. Mrs. Freeman actually *did* cry when he handed her an envelope with a thank-you card and cash.

That tender moment soon dried up. The Freeman family had grown sick and tired of hearing about the Adams family. Hustle couldn't boast enough about all the *stuff* they had, as though simply by having been in the midst of it, *he'd* owned it. Yeah, they had bank, *mad* bank judging from the house and furniture and games. Bling was one thing, but their *style* was tight too. Plus, they had servants, *white* ones. And the food was off tha hook. And the dope doorbell. The Adamses were straight-up *legit*, no frontin' necessary.

The television was turned on to the grand finale of *The Apprentice*, where the business tycoon Donald Trump selects the winning contestant who will get to work seventeen-hour days in one of his companies.

"Hook me up," said Ride, stretched out on the floor next to Hustle, who was describing Spence's entertainment system. "When *I* get a dinner invite?"

"When the Knicks win a NBA Championship."

Ride was a Knicks fan. "Why you gotta disrespect my team? They comin' back, you'll see."

Mr. Freeman reminded Hustle not to forget on whose backs America was built. "Black folks' sweat and blood is what made those fortunes for all these rich white people . . . these Adams people's company, the Trump dynasty, the Rockefeller empire . . ."

"Uh-uh, Pops, Damon Dash and Jay-Z made Roc-a-Fella."

"Boy," said Mrs. Freeman from her place on the couch, "just be quiet if you got nothing worth saying."

His father went on. "Without all that free African slave labor this country wouldn't—"

"Awww, man . . ." said Ride.

"Awww, man, *what*?" Mr. Freeman frowned.

"I'm just sayin' I ain't about all that."

"All *what*?"

"You know, all that Shaka Zulu–*Roots*–slavery drama. The way I sees it, they slaved, they got whipped, they died. It was messed up, but that was then. I'm livin' now."

Manley Freeman, Sr., glared at Manley Freeman, Jr., as if struggling with a powerful urge to beat him black and blue. Ride was a typical teenager. He took great pleasure in provoking his parents, getting a rise out of them. And a rise is exactly what he got, as his mother rose to her feet, walked over to him, and smacked him upside the head.

"You have to be the *biggest* bonehead this side of stupidity!"

"*Ow!* Wassup with the violence, Ma, why you gotta *hate*?"

In the commotion, the family missed the moment when Trump declared "You're hired!" to a stunned black novelist who'd earned a business degree after her writing career flopped.

25

JEANNETTE REMEMBERED FROM URBAN DESIGN CLASS THAT there were Romans atop the Grand Central Terminal. Mercury, the god of commerce and travel, stood near a clock, flanked on one side by Hercules and on the other by Minerva, the Roman goddess of wisdom and protector of towns. But she was too close to the building to see the famous *Transportation* sculpture, no matter how far back she leaned. Mrs. Simpson craned her neck in the opposite direction, looking down at her outfit. She tugged at the fitted jacket again and again, as if the man *himself* was going to be there.

"I look okay? You sure we're on the right street? How's my hair? And isn't it just like me to forget my watch on the dresser? What time you got?"

"Nanna, you *so* need to chill. Relax! It's ten to, and the restaurant's right on Vanderbilt and you look beautiful. He *is* married, though."

They turned onto Vanderbilt Avenue, named for the railroad tycoon Cornelius Vanderbilt, who once described himself as being "insane on the subject of moneymaking" and who died in 1877 worth a hundred million dollars. That evening, a more modern millionaire was on the minds of Jeannette and her grandmother. Mrs. Simpson had a wicked obsession with the basketball legend Michael Jordan, whose restaurant was on the balcony of the terminal. The thought of even being in a room where Michael had been was almost too much for the fan to bear.

Inside the station, Jeannette immediately saw Hustle. "There he is!"

"Where? Oh my God! You see Michael?" Mrs. Simpson was almost hyperventilating.

"*Hustle*, Nanna! The one who invited us to dinner? You are *playin'* yourself tonight. Michael Jordan's not gonna *be* in the restaurant. He doesn't even *live* in New York."

They waved up at Hustle, laughing like a couple of kids.

Hustle wasn't wearing a do-rag. *Or* a cap. Jeannette realized she'd never seen his head before. He wore his hair cut close, like the singer Usher. They were seated right away in the popular steak house, its interior an open plain of polished mahogany and leather.

"It's nice of you to take us to dinner, Hustle, but, honey, look at these prices . . . Are you sure? Because I'd be more than happy to—"

"This *my* treat. I got paid for—" He avoided mention of the infamous song. "And Jeannette told me how you be getting your *fiend* on for Mike."

Mrs. Simpson blushed from ear to ear. "Get my *what* on? *Guuurl* . . ." she said through her teeth, squeezing Jeannette's wrist hard.

"Tsk, tsk, Grandma Nanna. Don't be getting all *project* up in here. This is a *nice* restaurant. And Michael could come dribbling by any time."

Over a well-seasoned filet mignon for Mrs. Simpson, and a charred and salted forty-four-ounce porterhouse that Hustle and Jeannette shared, they chatted about basketball, the weather, public high schools, Trump's new black apprentice.

Jeannette said, "Hustle really liked the poetry book you gave him, right, Hustle?"

"I'm glad. I hoped it would inspire you."

"It did. Poetry ain't, I mean aren't, my thing, but I liked a lot of it. I've been working on—"

Jeannette knocked his knee with hers under the table.

Rap music was not a suitable dinner topic, not with Nanna at least.

Mrs. Simpson coughed into the linen napkin. "I hope it's not . . ." She'd promised Jeannette to refrain from criticizing Hustle. She dropped the topic. Hustle, however, was already beatboxing into his fist.

This shorty make me wanna stop
my hoodlum ways and reach the top
but movin' gear be all I got
don't wanna hafta end up shot . . . whoa

my talk, my walk it got me marked
one look at me they call a cop
the ledge I'm on is one long drop
she look my way and light the dark . . . whoa

one day I'm gonna be real sharp
and rule just like the meanest shark
the cash to spend, the cars to park
then shorty see just how I rock . . . whoa.

His audience quietly clapped. Mrs. Simpson praised it as a "great improvement," Jeannette said *"all riiight."* He smiled.

"How're you gonna sit there and tell me you don't like

poetry?" asked Mrs. Simpson. "That *is* poetry. We read things like that in my class every week. You have more?"

"Yeah, but they under construction. I spit staccato-style with a real stripped downbeat like a lean Neptunes mix."

Mrs. Simpson had no idea what he was talking about but took his hand. "Hustle, you *got* something. *That's* good writing. You *can't* be the same boy who wrote 'Back-Seat Hoochie.' "

Hustle and Jeannette laughed until their sides hurt but wouldn't tell Mrs. Simpson why.

"Oh, keep your little joke to yourselves. You know what I want you to do, Hustle? I want you to type up all your poems, raps, whatever you want to call them . . . If you don't have a computer, Jeannette can do it at her job . . ."

"Easily," said Jeannette, her heart racing. Nanna was *liking* him.

". . . and get them to me. I think they'd really interest a colleague of mine."

Jeannette asked him if he planned to make a new demo.

"Not right off the bat. I'ma chill for now, write more rhymes. I'm not feelin' the business end of it right now. I might break different, hook up a mix tape and sell it directly to people."

"Well, that's up to you. Just get me your poems," said Mrs. Simpson, tilting her head to the side. "Aight, *dawg*?"

26

WILD-EYED, SCREAMING STUDENTS EXPLODED OUT OF ALL the doors of George Clemens High School. There was no alienated shooter at their backs, no black smoke in the air, no swollen rats in the cafeteria. It was simply the last day of summer school.

Cheering to the skies, Ride took Sandie Justino's hand and raised it high like a referee with a victorious prizefighter.

"Free at last! Free at last!" squealed the girl, jumping up and down jingling bracelets and beads. "Thank God almighty, we are free at last! Just like King pro*claimed*! *Yaaaaaay!*"

"That ain't it, Sandie. What the man *said* was 'Why can't we all just get along?' "

He'd been hittin' on the cute Latina all summer but had gotten nowhere. She *did* let him in a side door every day, though. That way, he could stay *strapped* without running afoul of weapons detectors and patdowns. Folks be crazy, and he needed protection. In return, she got his protection from the school's "Chola-wannabe" gang girls.

The joy of the moment erased all such concerns. Laughing, she snatched her hand away. "You spent the whole summer in school, and you still come out *muy estúpido*. I meant *Martin Luther* King, not Rodney!"

Ride pretended like he knew. "Ha ha, you know I got jokes. Like I don't know the 'we shall overcome' crew. Come on, girl, get real!"

"Yeah, right, papi, *whatever*. Good luck in September, 'cause, *honey*, you gon' *need* it!" She ran towards a group of girlfriends.

"Damn!" said Ride, kicking the ground. He *did* know about all that, the civil rights dudes in suits getting hit with eggs . . . Anyway, *he* was down with them New Black Panthers who rocked *AK-47s* on *they* marches. Now *they* was dope.

"Don't be thinking *too* hard, your head might bust."

Hustle had been cruising around when he heard the cheers.

"Man, what *you* doin' near a school? What's next, Bill Cosby poppin' up in a 50 Cent video?" He *did* have jokes.

"That's real funny. Come here"—Hustle grabbed him by the neck and pressed his fist against Ride's nose—"wanna say hello to my little friend?"

"Bring it, H!"

"It's brought!"

The impromptu boxing match wasn't even noticed as everywhere giddy kids jumped, ran, shrieked, danced, ecstatic to be done with school. They lingered outside, savoring the moment, drawing it out as long as possible. A boom box appeared, and in minutes the whole sidewalk was transformed into a club. People in the projects nearby leaned from windows to bounce to the music, some ran downstairs to join in. From John Legend's gospel-tinged soul to Mariah's smooth dance grooves to The Game's gangsta flava, there was a sound for every taste, and it all tasted good. But it was the hip-hop remix of Me'Shell NdegéOcello's racy funk anthem "Pocket," with its Tweet soul and Redman flow, that turned the party *out*.

Hustle was talking with the guy who'd put together the music, and Ride had gotten Sandie to dance with him. Neither they nor anyone else took note of two girls watching from a dark car. Then came a *Pop! Pop! Pop! Pop!* faster than the brain could figure out that the sounds *weren't* fireworks. People couldn't trample each other fast enough. Hustle dropped to his knees behind a concrete wall. Ride crouched at a fire hydrant with Sandie, who was frozen with panic. The shooters' car screeched away before he'd been able to pull out his own "protection." But a greater protector was on duty that day. The only injuries were the cut hands, bruised knees, and twisted ankles of people who fell or were pushed out of the way. Police later arrested the girls, who said they were just "messin' " with people "for fun."

Hustle and Ride walked for blocks before they'd shaken off their jitters. Food seemed like a good idea. Hustle said he'd treat.

The waitress asked if they wanted dessert.

"Dessert?" responded Ride, reading the name on her uniform. "Who eat dessert after a banana split, *Felicia*? Ice cream *is* dessert."

"*Excuuuse* me, but I am doin' my *job*. There is *no* need to get all stank." She rolled her eyes and switched away.

Ride managed a weak laugh. But he was out of jokes. He felt the same way he did after Double Fo' got shot— uptight and stressed.

"That was the *max* of wack. I didn't know *where* the shots was comin' from until they sped off. Hadn't even looked *their* way. Who expect shorties to be shootin'? That was my second time coming close to . . . *man!* They say three strikes, you're out."

Hustle listened, feeling sick himself. He was no stranger to flying bullets, but the hundredth shoot-out was as terrifying as the first, if only because it could be the last.

"Don't sweat it like that, we all at the mercy of whatever go down, whenever it go down. It could be somebody's first time, they second time, third, fourth . . . tenth . . . it don't matter. You just gotta know how to keep your head low, don't attract nothing to you. You know what the inmates say?"

Ride was folding, unfolding, and refolding a paper napkin into an airplane. "What?"

"Heat draw heat."

"*Black* folk draw heat. Get on the subway at 125th when it be real hot outside . . ." Now he *did* laugh.

"Truedat. But that ain't what they mean. Nobody really know how it work, but it seem like that Wild West mess happen when a dude's armed. Almost everybody I met on the inside had caught some kinda gun charge, and that's why they say, heat draw heat. Even if I wasn't on probation, I wouldn't pack. I got too much to do to be taking chances. Think about it, knothead."

"So then the whole school musta been strapped since they *all* got shot at. Right. And *I'm* a knothead."

"You trippin' thinking a piece keep you safe. You wasn't safe today now, was you? If them girls coulda aimed— I bet you *anything* the kick sent all they rounds in the trees—we might not even be sitting here. Hotheaded as you can be, suppose a dude bump you, step on your sneakers, dis you . . . and you pull your weapon? You gonna draw heat. When you shoot at people, they shoot back. *That's* what I mean."

Ride threw the plane at Hustle's forehead.

Hustle put down money for the check.

"You ain't nothin' but a little kid, ain't you, *Maaanley*? We outta here, let's go."

The shooting was all over the news. When they got home, Ride's mother threw her arms around him. His father patted his back.

"I was so worried! There was a shooting at your school. The news said it was some kind of girl gang initiation thing. Thank God no one was killed! You were probably gone by then, right? It happened around five."

She held on to his arm as if vowing not to let him out of her sight ever again. Even though he was standing in front of her, she needed to reassure herself that her only child had been nowhere *near* harm's way.

There was no point bugging her out more than she already was. "Yeah . . . uh . . . I heard about it just now when we was in the ice cream shop and a lady was talking about it. But do y'all really see me hanging around school after it's over? And on my last day too? Ha ha."

"Heh heh" was Hustle's way of affirming Ride's story without having to lie outright.

There was a collective sigh of relief.

"It *is* your last day, I forgot." Mr. Freeman threw an arm around Ride's shoulder. "Good job, son. You'll get there."

Most of the night Ride lay awake watching whatever was on the television.

27

A MIGHTY RUCKUS FILLED STREET SAGE ACADEMY, THE
last hope of many near-dropouts who were trying to
make school work for them. Mr. Peters, wearing his sig-
nature shirt, tie, and khakis, brought the class to order.
Well, eventually. First, he clapped his hands twice. "Class!
. . . People!" This only amplified the racket of voices, cell
ring tones, and scraping chairs. He banged a ruler repeatedly, and pointlessly, on a desk. He opened the classroom
door and, using all his strength, slammed it shut with a
deafening bang. That brought the noise down to a tolera-
ble buzz.

"Sorry for the interruption, folks, but alternative
school is still *school*. Now take your seats. Not on her *lap*,
Kea, your *own* seat. Rockee, cut it out! This is *language*

arts, not martial arts. Feet belong on the floor. C'mon, guys, don't embarrass me, we have visitors today."

When Anita Simpson had shown him Hustle's written work, Mr. Peters phoned the Freeman house and invited him to speak at the school. True to form, Hustle haggled and bartered. No speechin', just spittin'. And his homeboy Ride was coming too. And they was gonna need lunch. And not in no cafeteria either. The educator agreed to everything, complimenting Hustle's "entrepreneurial spirit." But no, there would be no car or limo service and no two-hundred-dollar payment. Street Sage was a free, private school that survived on donations.

The visitors were scoping the scene from the back of the classroom. Ride wore his usual Phat Farm baggies and giant T-shirt. Hustle had bought a FUBU set of prefaded black jeans and a polo shirt with black and beige stripes. On his feet, he wore beige New Balance sneakers and, up top, a do-rag and NYFD cap, both black. His outfit was *clean* and his work memorized.

" 'Sup, y'all," he said.

"Yo," said Ride, with what he thought was *emcee attitude*.

Heads turned. " 'Sup," a few kids responded.

During Joe Peters's career as a high school teacher, libraries were shut as reading scores declined, gym classes ditched as students grew fat, and fun classes in music and art scrapped. Public schools were receiving no money for anything—except more police. So the NYU grad, who had a degree in ethnomusicology, opened his own school in a community center on the Lower East Side.

The student body was almost equally divided between black and Hispanic kids, the majority, and counted a growing number of white kids. The average age was seventeen, Hustle's age. But age wasn't all they had in common with him. Many of them knew the streets but not their parents. For all of them, school had been a bust. And, of course, urban culture was in full effect—the *rag* and the *sag*, the slanted cap and the love of rap.

"Last week Lady Tee-Tee and MC Biscotte stopped by to help us write rhymes and put them to different beats. To some, that's rap. To me, it's spoken poetry laid down to music. Who was one of the early pioneers of that form of expression, some call him the original rapper? Anybody remember?"

"I do, Joe," volunteered a boy near the back. "Gil Scott-Heron."

"Good memory, Jamal. And his most famous poem is . . . ?"

A girl held up a finger. " 'The Revolution Will Not Be Televised'—1970."

"*Yes*, Lani, excellent!"

He pointed out the "two gentlemen" in the back. "Today, we have Harlem's own Double H and MC Ride. Hustle is going to share with us his work, which you will hear derives from that same tradition."

Hustle stood, and his hands became Italian, dancing to the words. "All eyez on me is what I like to see, I'm writing since I'm three"—he was in the zone, *his* zone— "and my style is free."

Then he recited a rat-a-tat freestyle that drew *whoa*s and *ooooo*s.

"With clever wordplay fake emcees diss-play the next-to-nothin' they have to say, today's Black Light Special: buy one M&M peanut, get a free 50 Cent snack, doctored up to be triple Kmart(yr)-friendly, but my verse is terse, ain't no refuge from my deluge, cops need a warrant to stanch my torrent."

The class clapped, led by Ride. Mr. Peters invited the students to ask the visitors questions. A pencil-thin student raised her hand.

"Why all the girls in rap videos have to be half-naked hoochies and act all nasty like they in a porno?"

" 'Cause it's *rap*!" answered Ride, "and what's rap with-out—"

Before he could finish the girl said, "Crap."

Hustle was transported back to Sheepshead Bay, to Nanna's anger and Jeannette's embarrassment. He knew what *they'd* say—and maybe they'd be right. But he didn't want to come off *soft* in front of everybody.

"Personally, I ain't got a problem with nasty, *heh heh*."

"Chébranna makes a good point, guys," said Mr. Peters. "We all know the videos . . . women in thongs, bikinis, and teeny shorts bumping, grinding, and bouncing. I saw a video where one was literally standing on her head doing a split."

"Eeeew!"

"Stank!"

"But you probably *don't* know about COOL, the Crew of Outraged Ladies. It's a group that condemns using degrading images of females, especially black and Latina, to sell music. Their slogan is 'Don't believe the hype.' Has anyone ever heard of Hype Williams?"

No one had.

"Well, you all know his work because he's directed hundreds of rap and R & B videos. He peaked in the nineties, being the first to put what Chébranna calls 'half-naked hoochies' in music videos. A lot of folks see him as the Patient Zero in a plague that has spread internationally. COOL stages high-profile protests at video shoots. One of their more outrageous actions was to drag a video director from his trailer, buck naked, and videotape him being pelted with cow dung to chants of 'No more bullshit!' "

The kids howled with laughter.

"Oh, snap!"

"Whoa."

"That's *craaazy!*"

For the next forty minutes there was discussion, writing, and reciting. Everyone shared their work with the class, even the teacher, who was voted "Worst Wack Jack" for his line "my stomach *rumble* sometime . . . it make me *wonder* how to fill up all this *hunger* . . . hun, hun-hun-hun-hun." Hustle was voted "Best New Jack."

Nobody dissed, nobody dogged, nobody mocked. It wasn't tolerated. Besides, they'd all been there and done that in their old schools. Calling people out, putting each other down was lame. Respect, encouragement, support, that was cool. And no one needed or relished it more than this group of teenagers on whom almost everybody had given up.

Alphabet City was crawling with the hungry. At Joe Peters's favorite deli, customers shouted sandwich requests over the counter. He ordered lox on a bagel for himself, pastrami on rye for Hustle, and bologna on white for Ride. In Tompkins Square Park they sat on the semicircular benches in the shade of the towering Hare Krishna Tree, where in 1966 Swami Prabhupada led his followers in the first stateside chanting session of the famous Hare Krishna song. For some, this was a musical moment as seminal as the 1979 release of the first successful rap record, "Rappers Delight."

A round-the-clock teacher, Mr. Peters kept lecturing.

Now he was on the history of the park. A sixties mecca for hippies and radicals, the park later became a crime-ridden haven for drug addicts. And in the late eighties police violently evicted the homeless and activists who'd symbolically made the park their own Tent City and riots broke out.

"Man, Mr. Peters—" said Hustle.

"Joe. We use first names at school."

"Okay . . . Joe. How you hold all that in your head, little details and dates and everything?"

"Yeah, how you do that? Hustle forgets my birthday on purpose so he don't have to give me nothing." At that moment, a scrawny black squirrel scurried up Ride's leg.

"*Aaarrgh!* Get that thing offa me!"

It leapt on the ground and scooted away.

Hustle was doubled over, and Mr. Peters cracked up too.

A young woman with blue spiked hair, eyebrow piercings, holey jeans, and a dirty CBGB T-shirt stared at them, let out a loud guffaw, shrugged, and walked away.

"These street kids," said Mr. Peters, watching her, "you wonder how they manage out here, especially the girls." His dark eyes grew even darker as the faces of kids he *hadn't* been able to save floated to mind. He drew his focus back to the present.

"To answer the question, if you care, you remember.

It's as simple as that. Take rhymes, for example. You remember them because you care about the words, the ideas, the message. They inspire you and you inspire others. Which brings me to something that's been on my mind all morning, in fact, ever since Anita talked to me about you."

"Anita?" asked Hustle.

"Anita Simpson. Nanna?"

"Oh . . . Nanna!"

"We both think you should enroll at Street Sage."

Hustle didn't even have to think about it. "Nah, man, school and me didn't—"

"Just hear me out. You're not dumb, quite the contrary. And you have some real writing ability. I watched you this morning. You fit in, you were comfortable, engaged . . . I think you even liked it."

Hustle stomped his foot at a pigeon, which took off in a panic.

"Listen, Joe, I appreciate where you coming from, but the nerdy schoolboy thing's not for me. I wanna be a *rapper*. They proof that you don't need school to get paid. Most of them even got criminal records. But they millionaires, livin' *extra* large. What I need school for?"

"Yeah, *boyeee* . . ." Ride held up his fingers to form an H. "Double H up in the *house*."

Mr. Peters had heard the same speech a million times. And he gave the same reply. "You need school because an education gives you options. Alternatives. A backup plan if need be. And you'll be smarter at *whatever* you do, be it rap, sports, or cleaning teeth. Why *not* learn? There's no rule that says a recording artist *has* to be uneducated. Let me give you some examples: Chuck D, high school graduate, was studying graphic design at Adelphi University when he formed Public Enemy. Nas, high school graduate, attended North Carolina A & T State College. Queen Latifah, high school graduate, studied at the Borough of Manhattan Community College. Ludacris, high school graduate, attended Georgia State University in Atlanta. Jennifer Lopez, high school graduate, spent twelve years in Catholic school. Diddy graduated from a private Catholic boys' school and studied business at Howard University. Usher, Alicia Keys, Eve . . . all high school graduates. Russell Simmons and Rick Rubin were both in college when they founded Def Jam Recordings. Young MC has a degree in economics from USC in Los Angeles. Pranksta studied—"

"*All right, all right,* man!" Pranksta was not a name Hustle was in the mood to hear. "I *gets* the point. I wasn't up on all that, and I prop *all* of them, they get mad respect from me. I'm not really *against* learning . . . this girl I hang with, she go to a prep school, and a homey of mine do too. When I *was* in school it just wasn't—"

Ride laughed. "Hustle ain't been in a school since Hammer had money."

172

One good thing that came from MC Hammer's bankruptcy, thought Mr. Peters, was that it taught kids the importance of not just getting money but holding on to it. He directed his next question to Ride.

"And how're *your* grades?" The kid had all the signs of a future dropout and clearly needed an academic alternative. And maybe if one of them enrolled, the other would. "You said back in class that you were in summer school? Left back once already? Making up classes? I'd say you're having some trouble as well. You might also do better in a different style school."

Ride tuned him out. He threw his head back, emptied the last drops of soda into his mouth, and shot the plastic bottle in a high arc towards the trash can. It went in.

"*Yesss!* Two points."

"I want you *both* to consider it. We have rolling admissions, meaning you can start tomorrow if you like. A private school can do that. The other students are there to back you up. You'll be ahead of the game come September." He stood. "In any case, thanks for coming in today. You gave the class a lot, Hustle . . . and I think *we* have a lot to give you. Call me. Call Anita. Think about it."

Mr. Peters looked at his watch.

"Oh, and one last thing . . . Tupac studied ballet at the Baltimore School for the Arts."

The teacher disappeared down the street. Hustle and Ride tossed crumbs at pigeons. Joe *had* to be joking, they agreed. Tupac "Thug-for-Life" Shakur doing ballet? For them, the story couldn't possibly be true. But it was.

"In tights and everything?" asked Mr. Freeman incredulously. Ride had just told his father what Mr. Peters said about the rapper. Mr. Freeman was a big fan and simply could not imagine Tupac doing a Swan Lake pas de deux.

The rapper in tights didn't interest Mrs. Freeman "one iota," as she put it. The school program Hustle had described was what had her dreaming. Maybe a different, smaller school *would* be a good change for Lee, and a new start for Eric.

"If Man had stayed in school," she said, "or me too for that matter, our life would certainly have been better . . . better jobs, a better home. But we were know-it-alls, just like you two now. What happens, Eric, if you *don't* end up a rich fool with one of those ugly Hummers and a lot of jewelry, *then* what? And your pal Manley over here, don't even get me started! He'll be twenty years old and still in high school clowning in the back row. I think you should do it."

"So do I," said Mr. Freeman. He paused. "But his feet . . . no way Tupac could get those big feet in them little slippers. I think that teacher was pulling somebody's leg."

Hustle was also thinking, but not about Tupac Shakur's ballet moves. Joe was an okay dude. The class *was* pretty cool. The Freemans wanted him to go. He didn't even have to *ask* Jeannette's opinion. Or Mrs. Simpson's. It wasn't like he was enlisting or anything, he thought. He and Ride talked about school late into the night, weighing the few pros and the many cons. Ride hated the school he was in and thought he'd at least have more fun at Street Sage, if nothing else. In the end, the decision came down to Hustle's assurance that they could always drop out if it was wack. They agreed to give Street Sage Academy a try.

28

ON SALE SIGNS ADORNED THE WINDOWS OF HARLEM'S shops and stores. Even the smallest storefront "beauty nooks" were offering "Back-to-School" hair-braiding specials. Parents leading children by one hand and grasping school supplies in the other hurried from store to store, chasing bargains. It was the time of year, the end of summer, when department store chains hired extra security to thwart shoplifters, particularly fashion-minded, poor students gearing up for school.

A pair of girls strolled 125th Street window-shopping and chatting. It was their last weekend in New York City before they would return to the sloping hills of the Fletcher School campus.

"Why are all these people *running?*" asked Willa, who'd just been bumped by a hefty woman wielding massive shopping bags. "The sales *do* continue right through Labor Day, *helloooo.*"

Jeannette rolled her eyes.

"I know it's hard for you to imagine, being so *bourgeois* and all, but we poor folk get *real* excited when we can finally afford at sale time what you casually buy *whenever* the Great Shopping Spirit moves you."

"I'm *crying,*" said Willa sarcastically. "Poor folk shouldn't waste their limited resources on expensive sneakers, shapeless jeans, and cheap doodads they really don't need. Look! There's Nanna coming out of the ninety-nine-cent store!"

"Hi, Lillian," said Jeannette to the bag lady pushing a cart piled high with rags, torn papers, and recyclable plastic containers.

"Don't you *take* my mother's name in vain!" warned Willa.

They were a few blocks away from the Crib, where a very special event was scheduled to take place. The owner, a friend of Joe Peters, was holding a fund-raiser for the Street Sage Academy. Rumors had everyone short of a resurrected Elvis showing up—Def Poetry Jam scouts, BET's *106 & Park* producers, Mariah Carey, KRS-One, Alicia Keys, Caushun, even Celine Dion's name was mentioned. Most of the whispered "surprise guests" were fantasies. But a half dozen performers were confirmed *definites*. They were the school's six most talented students. And among that group was a brand-new student, Eric "Double H" Samson.

Every table was taken. People were leaning against walls. Up above hung a "Street Sage Academy Presents Slammin' Slammers" banner. Copies of the students' "hip-hop-inspired verse" were for sale, alongside T-shirts and coffee mugs. Jeannette scanned the room for Spence, who'd promised to save them seats. She spotted him sitting with an older couple at a front table.

"There he is," she said, and they nudged their way through the crowd, drawing the predictable grumbles.

"Where they think *they* goin'?"

"Y'all need to switch your tails right back to the *back*!"

"No they *not* gon' stand up there and block *my* view."

Willa whispered to Jeannette, "Your homegirls are getting a little rambunctious."

"I have nothing to do with those chickens. You sure they're not your cousins?"

Laughing, they joined Spence and the Freemans.

"Hi, Willa. Hi, Jeannette," said Spence. He gestured to the couple. "Meet Hustle's godparents, Lena and Manley Freeman."

Jeannette blushed. Willa noticed and chuckled. The girls sat down.

Spence regretted Nate's absence. "He *so* should be here. When does he get back, Willa?"

Willa checked her watch. "In exactly five days, seven hours, and twenty minutes."

They were still laughing and talking when Ride's voice boomed over the mic. "*Wadduuuup*, writers, readers, good-deeders, and rhyme-breeders."

His parents waved excitedly. He smiled and tapped his chest with his fist.

"I'm Ride Freeman, and we here to drum up some donations for my future school, Street Sage Academy, so we can get a liberry and books to put in it and a computer. And Joe need a new tie."

Laughter filled the room.

"Nah . . . y'all know I got jokes. As for me, I used to be a lefty . . . left back and left out . . . and now I'm trynna get right. So without further *to do*, as they say, we gon' kick this thing off with my own *homeboyeee* straight off the One-Two-Eight, make some *noise* for Double H up in this house . . . Harlem Hustle!"

Hustle walked onstage and sat on a wooden stool. The house lights went down, and the room vanished into darkness as a single beam fell across him. He could see no one and felt peaceful, like he was home rapping in his room, alone. Over a stripped-down, lean beat, he delivered his staccato-style verse:

To rappers, jackers, finger-snappers
who (w)rap us, jack us, and brain-snatch us
with gang-banging, slang-slinging, bling-blinging
I ask
does trigga rhyme only with nigga?

Go, Black Boy, it's ya birthday
so give birth to a new day
Richard Wright talked right, right?
did that make him white? aight
So stop frontin' and get backin'
up off
the booty-crackin', car-jackin', ill-wackin'
way you livin'.

Let's blow up, boom!
let's grow up, soon
our doom, it looms.
Uptown it go down
fellas hittin' red ground
for nothin'
Glock-rockin' awe-shockin' soldiers on the wrong
*   battleground*
ain't nothin'

the Five-O's, the P.O.'s, got us all on lockdown
we nothin'
the cell a small hell, his head spinnin' around
feel nothin'
full-grown home alone, no queen wearin' his crown
built nothin'
girls hollerin', moms cryin', they mouth making no
  sound
lived nothin'.

Let's blow up, boom!
let's grow up, soon
our doom, it looms.

What if her smile was the trigga to why you dig her?
what if a book was the trigga that made you think
  bigger?
what if a drunk drive was the trigga for you to quit
  liquor?
Again I ask
does trigga really *rhyme* only *with* nigga?
Stop.

The room was hushed. Then murmurs began softly
and grew louder. And all at once, as if his words had
reached their mark in slow motion, thunderous applause
and cheers erupted. Jeannette's voice was in his head—

when you're onstage . . . you better give the B.K. a big-up.
He kept his promise.

"Thanks, y'all. Thanks. And for my girl out there . . . Big up, Brooklyn. I'm out. Peace." And then Hustle did his rapper laugh.